# Vae Lycan

## Karon Evans

NEWMAN SPRINGS PUBLISHING
320 Broad Street
Red Bank, NJ 07701

First originally published by Newman Springs Publishing 2024

ISBN 979-8-89308-033-9 (Paperback)
ISBN 979-8-89308-034-6 (Digital)

Printed in the United States of America

# Chapter 1

# In the Beginning

In a world of vampires, werewolves, and humans, property lays its foot on the humans. Some of them are kings and queens. They rule their country with an iron fist. Some are rich and very wealthy and have their noses held high and mighty. The others are middle-class civilians, households that earn between two-thirds and double, day-in and day-out jobs. The unfortunate ones are the poor ones who sleep in the streets.

The Catholic church pastor sent the altar boy to sweep the dirt off the sidewalk from the poor and shoo them away. As the altar boy shooed the poor away, he felt trembling underneath his feet. He looked and noticed it's the Bright Light Soldiers marching down the street. They were under the orders of the Catholic church to protect the civilized people from vampires and werewolves. But not all humans received their protection, for some humans were slaves to the kings and queens of vampires. Most of them were mistreated and used to be fed on like cattle. These slave humans were left behind. No help will come for them, and vampires who are kings and queens are the elders, the powerful ones with remarkable abilities. Even their children who are born prince and princess, true-blooded vampires, possess incredible strength and abilities.

Unlike vampires, werewolves do not believe in the fashion of slavery, they live by spirituality and one with nature. Some of them are kings and queens; they rule their land. Other werewolves live in packs, staying to themselves and loving a good hunt. The kings and queens are the elderly, powerful werewolves; they are faster and stronger. Born werewolves are stronger than bitten werewolves; most bitten werewolves are soldiers to the kings. Some humans live among them in peace and safety behind the walls. They work, pay their taxes, and raise their families. Werewolves do not believe in discrimination; even women who are human work under the king to earn their coin.

Werewolves and vampires do not cross each other. It's forbidden for a werewolf and a vampire to even sexually twine with each other. *You will be killed!* It is a death sentence for two different species to be romantically involved with each other.

But this story doesn't begin here with them. To understand this story, we must start from the very beginning: the king of all vampires and werewolves, Vlad the Impala, Dracula, son of the dragon, son of the devil from Transylvania. The story begins with him in the year AD 576. To protect his people from a tax collector who was invading his land of war, Dracula traded his soul to a demon who was cursed to live in a cave by the devil who betrayed him.

When the empire struck war on Dracula's land, the enemy chased his wife up the stairs. When she reached the top of the castle, the enemy dared to push her off the ledge. Before they did such, Dracula swarmed in like a lightning bolt, killed the enemy. His wife was by the ledge, lost her balance, and fell off the ledge. Dracula leaped off the ledge and flew, trying to save his wife. He didn't make it in time to catch her. Dracula won the war but lost his beloved, named Elisabeta of Transylvania. They had a son, and he was next in line for the throne; his name is Parkinson. And then Dracula was gone; no record of him ever existed.

A century has passed since then, and rumors have spread of a dark creature terrorizing the night. But one night, a beautiful young lady, who is interested in science, stumbled upon Dracula's castle. "Hello, hello!" she said as she opened the door and walked inside. Dracula hid in the shadows like a quiet mouse, and she said, "I was told by one of the villagers I can find books of knowledge of science here." She continued to walk through the castle as Dracula continued to stalk her in the shadows. Then she said, "Oh, I hope, I'm not intruding." Dracula pierced behind her. Before he attacked her, he noticed she looked just like his wife, like a reincarnation of her. He marveled, almost in tears; his eyes were in a daze. He tapped her on the shoulder and said, "Excuse me, but how may I help you?"

She turned around and said, "Oh, you startled me."

He bowed to her and said, "My apologies, my name is Valid Dracula. How may I help you?"

She said, "Oh yes, nice to meet you, Mr. Valid. My name is Cleo, Cleo Brown. I am very interested in your books of science, medicine, herbs, and philosophy."

Dracula asked, "And why is that, may I ask?"

"To help people," Cleo answered.

He said, "God loves his people, for he died for them on the cross. Come with me, I'll show you the way." He took her to the library, and when they arrived, she was amazed at the thousands of books she sees. She spun around in joy and said, "This is incredible."

Dracula looked at her with a smile and said, "I'm glad you're pleased."

## One year had passed

She stayed in the castle, helping the villages of the land with the knowledge she learned of medicine and herbs, healing the sick. As she was helping one of the villagers, Dracula looked at her and found her desirable. She noticed him looking at her and smiles back with butterflies in her stomach. For she didn't see a monster or a vampire, not even a dark creature of the night, but a man with a good heart. They married, and four years later, she was pregnant. Nine months had passed, and she was giving birth. Three deaconesses assisted in helping with her labor.

"The baby is crowning, keep pushing, my lady." She pushed and yelled in pain. "The baby is coming, almost there." The baby was finally here. "It's a boy!"

The other assistant said, "It's a beautiful baby boy."

One of the deaconesses left the room to inform Dracula of the good news. He was anxious, drinking a glass of wine, waiting patiently in the dining room by the fire with his assistant Igor. "It's a boy, my lord," she said when she entered the room.

His eyes sparkle with joy. "A boy?" he said.

The second deaconess came and said to her, "Quick! We need your help. Another one is coming."

Dracula was so shocked, he dropped his wineglass. "Another one?" he said. Both deaconesses head back toward the delivery room. When they both arrived, the second baby was already crowning. "Push, my lady, push!"

She yelled and pushed.

"It's another boy," the deaconess said as she was holding the second baby boy.

Suddenly, after she gave birth the second time, the breathing of Dracula's wife was very low; she was bleeding heavily. They could not stop the bleeding.

Moments later, Cleo Brown, Dracula's wife, had died during childbirth. The deaconess carried the twin boys out of the room, heading toward Dracula. She entered the room. "Two identical, twin healthy boys," she said as she handed him his new twin baby boys.

He smiled at them with joy in his eyes. "They are beautiful just like their mother. I shall name them Cain and Abel. And how is my boys' mother?"

The deaconess bowed her head down and said not a word.

"I asked of my wife."

She spoke not a word once more, for she was afraid to answer. Dracula handed his twin boys to Igor, and he asked the deaconess with bass and anger in his voice, "I asked about my wife, and I will not ask a fourth time!"

She finally had the courage to answer him and said, "She didn't make it, my lord. I am so sorry. We couldn't stop the bleeding, we did everything we could." She spoke as if she's in frightened tears.

Dracula was angry, his eyes were fire red. "Everything you could?" He pushed her out of the way and ran toward the room. He burst through the door like a madman. The two other deaconesses, trembled and scared, quickly stepped away from the bed. He rushed toward his wife, grabbed her, and screamed and screamed in pain and tears.

## Three years later

Dracula had been in a deep depression since the loss of his wife. He paid little attention to his boys, though he loved them deeply. But he couldn't even bear to look at them because all he saw was their mother in his boys. He spent most of his time drinking a glass of blood wine, sitting in his chair by the fire. Igor dared not bother him. The servants of the castle took care of the boys.

One day, the boys were in their room wrestling with each other, being aggressive. "Okay, boys, that's enough horseplay," the servant said as she entered the room. The boys paid her no mind and continued to wrestle. Cain transformed into a vampire with wings, pointy ears, gray skin, incredible strength and speed (faster than a falling star), and possessed the ability to sonic scream. Abel transformed into a werewolf; he was stronger than his brother and fast like lightning. He also possessed the ability to thunderclap. However, neither of them was stronger than their father, for he was the king of kings of all vampires and werewolves. No one was near his strength.

The servant watched them transform. "Oh my goodness," she said. She immediately ran toward Dracula to tell him what she had just witnessed.

"My lord, my lord."

He looked at her as if he were annoyed and asked, "What is it?"

"It's the boys, come quick."

He got up from his chair and headed toward the boys' room. When he arrived, he saw his boys' transformation. Cain, the one who turned into a vampire, was flying in the air, using his sonic scream at his brother. Abel, the one who turned into a werewolf, was dodging his brother's attacks and jumping off the wall, using his thunderclaps at his brother.

"Extraordinary," Dracula said.

*Eighteen years later*

Cain and Abel were racing through the woods. "You're not faster than me, brother!" Abel said.

"Unless I fly." Cain turned into his flying vampire form and began flapping his wings into the sky.

"Cheater," Abel said. He turned into his werewolf form and ran like the speed of lightning. As they were racing each other, they came across a woman being raped by nine soldiers. Six of them stood there and watched and laughed as they were drinking, while the poor woman was being taken advantage of. It was entertaining for them.

"Disgraceful," Abel said.

"Let's kill them," Cain said.

The woman screamed for help. The boys swarmed the soldiers; they ripped their heads off and tore their arms off. One soldier was terrified. He got on his hands and knees and begged for his life. Cain picked up the soldier's sword and stabbed him through the mouth. "Now you are forgiven." The soldier's blood covered the woman's body from the splatter. She was so scared, she could not say a word, as she stood there in shock. Finally, she had the courage to take off and run. They returned to their normal form.

"Oh, you're very welcome!" Cain said as the woman was running from them.

"That was rude of her," Abel said.

"Must have been the way you look, brother. You are the ugly one," Cain said.

"Umm, I thought the same thing as you," Abel said.

They walked on the path back toward the castle, and as they journeyed, Abel said, "I have always been curious, brother."

"Curious of what?"

"How are you able to be in the sun and not burn like father, and not even need blood to drink?" Abel asked.

Cain shrugged his shoulders and answered, "I guess it's our human side."

"Umm," Abel said.

"But I tell you what, brother. We should kill half of these humans, enslave the rest, and rule over them under our belt. They are ignorant people, murderers, rapists, and killing each other for pleasure. Rulers, empires, and politicians playing their sick children's game. Getting rich off the poor. I say we should give them a new direction. Our direction," Cain said.

"I hear you, brother. But I disagree. If you do this, you are no different from them. That is not the way. There are some good people in this beautiful world we live in," Abel said.

"Oh, yeah, who?" Cain said.

"Our mother," Abel said.

"Never met her, she died," Cain said.

"Don't be ignorant, there's human in you too. That's the darkness of our father in you talking," Abel said.

"The man has been missing for years, depressed over mother. Left us the castle and human services. The only toy we have around here to play with is Igor," Cain said.

"We do play tricks on him a lot," Abel said.

"Like that time we threw snakes on him," Cain said.

"He ran and trip down the steps," Abel said.

They both laugh. "Hahahaha!"

"But seriously, brother. I mean what I said. We should rule over these humans," Cain said.

"And I disagree. They should have their free will like ours," Abel said.

They both finally made it back to the castle, and Cain said, "And when that day comes, brother, don't you dare stand in my way." Cain turned into his flying vampire form and flew off into the sky.

*Fifteen years later*

There was a mighty ruler named King Victor Allen. He commanded one million soldiers under his sword, but the king was on his deathbed. When the king was in his room alone, lying in bed, looking pale, nearing the crossover life, Cain appeared in his room as a dark figure shadow with red eyes. The king thought he was an

7

angel, but he was a demon in disguise. Cain said to the king, "I've been watching you, great King Victor."

"Who are you?" the king said with a low, sick voice.

"Someone who can offer you eternal life. But you must submit to me and shall rule this world by my side, as my general, and I'm your lord and king. Do you accept?"

The king could barely speak, but he said, "Yes, my lord."

Cain bit his own wrist and told King Victor to drink his blood. The next day, the king rose from the bed. King Victor Allen was the first true, powerful turned bloodsucker vampire with abilities of lightning and telekinesis, but the king was nowhere near the strength of Cain.

A servant came into the king's room and saw the king walking on the wall. She said, "Oh my lord." The king attacked her, turning her into a vampire. Later that night, the king turned all his soldiers and servants into vampires. They were not as strong as King Victor and did not possess any abilities, for they were bitten vampires.

Days went by, and Cain offered immortality to eleven more kings to rule under him, and they submitted to Cain as their god. All eleven kings were strong and powerful, and each king possessed a different, unique ability. They also turned their servants and soldiers into bitten vampires.

Cain built his army and had all twelve kings as his generals. War began on the humans; Cain ruled them in his direction of life.

## As time passed

Ten kings who were humans rebelled against Cain's vampire army. They were having a gathering at a secret location to discuss the vampire war on humans. Abel also attended the gathering; he stood in the middle of the floor, and the words he spoke was, "My brother must be stopped at once!"

A king named Shakur stood up and the words he spoke were, "We accept the gifts of a werewolf from the true lycanthrope."

Another king stood up and said, "Yes, Werewolf King, we accept the gift."

All the kings stood up and yelled, "Aye!"

Abel took a dagger, cut his wrist, poured his blood into a cup, and told the ten kings to drink from this cup, "For this is the new covenant in my blood for a new beginning of werewolves." Each king drank this cup and turned into a werewolf and was able to turn at any given will. But the kings were not stronger or faster than Abel. The kings returned to their homeland and bit their soldiers, turning them into werewolves, and because they were bitten by werewolves, they were not as strong as the kings.

Weeks went by, and an all-out war began: vampires versus werewolves.

Abel confronted his brother and said to him, "Brother, you must stop at once. You have spilled innocent blood, you have caused enough pain and suffering."

Cain replied, "Shut your dog-breath mouth. You bark like a bitch in heat. You are weak. I'm the ruler of this world, the grandson of the devil. And you, my brother, choose to stand with the weaklings."

"No, brother, I stand with the righteous!"

"That's the human in you talking, how boring and pathetic."

Abel turned into his form and said, "Fight me, brother!"

Cain turned as well and said, "To the death!"

Cain flew in the air and used his sonic scream. Abel dodged out of the way like lightning and he jumped in the air, charging at Cain like a flying bullet. He struck at Cain, but Cain dodged the attack, causing Abel to miss. Cain grabbed Abel by the tail and spun him around and threw him into the ground. Cain flew down, charging at Abel, he dodged out of the way, and grabbed Cain by the ankle and threw him so hard, he was knocking down trees, like wrecking boulder. Cain quickly got up, and Abel swung with a right, a left, a right, and another left. Cain dipped each swing and grabbed Abel by the throat and picked him up and threw him in the air and punched him so hard, he flew half of a yard. Cain grabbed a sword off a dead soldier lying in dirty mud. Abel struggled to get up because he was dizzy, trying to shake it off. Cain quickly rushed toward his brother Abel, like the speed of a falling star he is, with the sword in hand. Cain was behind him; Abel turned around, and Cain stabbed him through the chest, and he whispered in his ear, "You may be stronger than me, brother, but you were never faster than me." Cain pulled the sword out. Abel died slowly; he held his chest, falling to the ground, and took his last breath. Cain killed his brother, Abel. He turned back into normal, then suddenly, a bright spirit of a woman appeared and hovered over Abel's dead body. Cain looked shock for he recognized the spirit woman, and he said, "This cannot be, Mother." He spoke in a trembling voice.

"Where is your Abel, thy brother?" she asked in a rhetorical question as she cried.

"Am I my brother's keeper?"

"Oh, look what you have done. The voice of your brother's blood is crying to the heavens from the ground, and now you are cursed."

"And my punishment, Mother?"

"I will mark your head with a dark mark. The world will know you killed your own brother. Your allies will turn against you, for you cannot be trusted. That is your curse, and as for your brother, his gift will be, his spirit will live on and be reborn through another lycanthrope, of a newborn child with a pure heart, that's stronger and even more powerful. Abel's gift is your curse." She turned Abel's body into ash, and his spirit flew into a star, then she marked Cain's head and said, "When the star is big and bright, Abel has been reborn." Then she vanished.

## Two years had passed since then

Cain continued with his world domination and slavery. His twelve vampire kings were having a secret meeting with the ten werewolf kings. They decided to stop killing each other and work together; they are disgusted. Cain's reign of terror must come to an end. They were planning how he can be stopped. The twelve vampire kings believe Cain can no longer be trusted.

"Cain must be stopped at once, we can no longer trust him. We are nothing but pawns in his plan," King Victor said.

"We agree, King Victor, with your words. But why do we need your help? And what peace do you offer between vampires and werewolves?" Wolf King Shakur said.

"You and I both know, Cain is one of the strongest ones, he is the son of Dracula. It will take all of us to bring down the mighty king. Vampire kings and wolf kings, collaborate as one! Knowing we set aside our differences to defeat Cain. It will be written in history," King Victor said.

"And what about human slavery?" the Wolf King asked.

"I don't believe in human slavery. I have no slaves for myself. But I do not speak for the other vampire kings on human slavery," King Victor said.

A few vampire kings stood up and spoke, "In due time, we shall free them."

"Then that leads me to my final question," Wolf King Shakur said.

"Speak your peace," King Victor said.

"What of the theory, if we kill Cain, don't all vampires turn back to normal? For when Cain killed Abel, we werewolves remained the same," Wolf King Shakur said.

"We already have a plan for him. Imprison him for all eternity. His prison will be so concealed, not even the sun will be able to shine upon him. Even as we speak, the prison is already being built, and only us kings here in this room would know of its location," King Victor said.

"Let's get started then," Wolf King Shakur said.

The meeting came to an end, and all the kings shook hands. As they were leaving the secret meeting, a vampire queen whispered to each other, saying, "We will never free the slaves."

"Agreed," said King Bombardment, who possesses the element of fire.

"Agreed," said King Move, who possessed the power to teleport himself and others.

"Agreed," said King Erode, who possesses the ability to control the weather.

"We must keep this from King Victor, for he is our law and too powerful for us to take on," said Queen Jayne. She possessed the power of manipulation and a whisper; she is a master of the sword.

"Agreed," said King Glacier, who possessed the ability to create, shape, and manipulate ice, water frozen into a solid state.

## Two weeks had passed since then

Cain was in his castle, sitting on his throne, unaware of the upcoming attack. As he was sitting on the throne, he felt trembling underneath his feet. He got up and looked out the window and noticed the werewolf kings heading toward his castle. He yelled to his guards, saying, "Guards! Get my kings' generals, immediately! We are being attacked."

The wolf kings stormed through the castle, killing the guards. They burst through Cain's door and attacked him on sight. The generals of Cain's vampire kings finally arrived, for they were already there hiding, and they killed the messenger guard.

"Let us end the reign of Lord Cain tonight!" King Victor said.

They rushed inside the castle and attacked Cain as well.

"What the hell are you doing?" Cain said as they were ganging up on him.

"Bringing you to an end," King Bombardment said as he threw fireballs at him.

"You bloody fucking traitors, I gave you eternal life!" Cain said in a very angry, raging voice.

"You gave us lies!" King Erode said as he used the weather of lightning to strike at him. They all continued to gang up on Cain, then Queen Jayne threw a chain around Cain. A mighty unbreakable chain bound him; he was unable to move.

"Damn bastards! I'll kill you all! Unhand me. Now!" Cain said in a frustrated voice.

"Oh, we have plans for you," Wolf King Shakur said.

They concealed his mouth so he wouldn't be able to use his sonic scream. They brought in a casket that locked from the outside. Cain wiggled like a worm as they picked him up and placed him inside the locked casket. The werewolf kings carried the casket out of the castle.

They traveled for eight days to Cain's prison. They finally arrived and kept him locked inside the casket; Cain's prison was built one hundred feet down a dark stairway in a sacred tomb. When they reached the end of the stairway, they opened two big locked doors and placed Cain inside his cell and locked the doors for all eternity. And above the tomb door, it's written with a warning, "Do Not Disturb This Evil."

Twenty years have passed since then, and a second war broke out, between werewolves and vampires, over the slavery of humans. The werewolf kings believed the humans should be free and to practice their Christian religion. But during the time of war, Wolf King Shakur died in battle; he was killed by Queen Jayne. And he had two younger adult sons in their very early twenties, named Gerald, who is the firstborn, and then Ka'Ron, who is the second-born. Long live the king! His second son, Ka'Ron, became the new werewolf king of Galloway. The war lasted just a little over a year, and the humans were now free. And a new beginning began; they were able to express their free Christian religion, and over the years, churches were built, and the Christian soldiers of the Bright Light emerged.

(Now we're all caught up, and the real story begins.)

# Chapter 2

# Prince Kaiden

*Thirteen years later*

A big bright star was shining in the middle of the sky, and a spirit came out of that star, floating in the midst of the night. A woman, who was a werewolf queen named Lawanda, was giving birth, and beside her was her werewolf king, Ka'Ron, who is King Shakur's second-born son. And four deaconesses were helping with the delivery of the birth. Their daughters, named Adrianna and Zy'Asiah, being nosy, were peeking through the crack of the door. And the spirit from the bright star hovered over the woman who was giving birth.

"This is the one, this baby boy, him and I shall be one. And blessed with my strength and abilities, with a new transformation of a lycanthrope, for I am Abel."

Prince Kaiden was born; you could hear his cries through the whole castle and the town of Galloway. And the spirit of Abel entered inside of baby Kaiden, his eyes turning brown.

"What shall we name him, my love?" King Ka'Ron asked.

She told her two daughters to come into the room.

"He's beautiful, Mother," the girls said.

"Yes, he is," Lawanda said as she was holding him. "We shall name him Kaiden. For *Kaiden* means companion, warrior, deriving from Arabic, Celtic. The name is popular in the Christian religion and means a 'loving companion' and 'warrior' who is affectionate and committed. For he was born in a world where war is a breath away between werewolves, vampires, and humans. Humans who use swords against us. Vampires who despise and see us not as equals. But he will be loved by some and be hated by many. And his love will overcome that hate. He will be feared and respected because of his bravery as a warrior. His name is Prince Kaiden."

"Inform my brother, Gerald, his nephew's name is Prince Kaiden," King Ka'Ron said to the deaconesses.

## Ten years later

Shymair was Kaiden's cousin on his mom's side of the family. Shymair's dad was Shummy; he was Kaiden's uncle-in-law. Shummy was the husband of Kaiden's aunt, Kim, and her sister was Queen Lawanda. Kim was King Ka'Ron's sister-in-law. And Shummy was the general of King Ka'Ron's army.

Jessica was Kaiden's childhood friend. Jessica and her mom were human. Jessica's mom was a servant in the castle. She oversaw the other twenty servants of the castle; they were not slaves. The humans of the land worked for peace, harmony, and coins. For all werewolves across the world believed slavery caused the second war.

Now on a beautiful day today, Kaiden, Shymair, and Jessica, all three of them were playing hide-and-go-seek in the castle. Kaiden was in the kitchen counting to ten. Shymair and Jessica went to go hide. Shymair quickly ran down the hallway, passing Zy'Asiah, who was Kaiden's second older sister. She said, "Slow down!"

He hid in the room of Kaiden's oldest sister, Adrianna, under her bed. "He's never gonna find me in here."

Jessica hid in the neighbor's boneyard.

"Ready or not, here I come," Kaiden said.

Adrianna walked into her room and heard someone laughing from under her bed. She looked under and saw Shymair and said, "*Get out!* Your big watermelon head!" Adrianna always called him that.

He ran out of the room, laughing. Kaiden saw him and said, "I see you, I'm going to get you." Kaiden ran after Shymair and tackled him to the ground. "Got you!"

"Hahahaha," they laughed together.

"Okay, you got me. Let's find Jessica," Shymair said.

"Okay."

Lord Gerald, who was Kaiden's uncle, walked by and said, "What are you boys up to?"

They both said, "Playing hide-and-go-seek."

"We're looking for Jessica," Kaiden said.

"Have you seen her?" Shymair asked.

"Now, boys, if I tell you, that would be cheating. But I will give you a hint."

"Okay," Shymair said.

"Ohhh. A hint," Kaiden said.

"What animal can you ride on its back, eat grass and hay, and sleep in a blank? Figure that out, and you have your answer," Lord Gerald walked away.

The boys thought and thought about the answer.

"I got it! I know where she is, follow me," Kaiden said.

They quickly rushed out of the castle and headed outside.

"She's in here, in the barn."

Kaiden opened the door and said, "I know you're in here."

They followed the sound of her laughing.

"There you are!" Kaiden said as he jumped on her, and Shymair jumped on her behind him.

"Okay, okay. You got me, let's play a different game," Jessica said.

Jessica's mother rang the bell and yelled out, "*Time for dinner!*"

"Let's play tomorrow, time to eat," Shymair said.

"I'm starving," Kaiden said.

"Me too," Jessica said.

The three of them rushed to the royal dining room. When they arrived, everyone else was already sitting at the royal long dinner table, and King Ka'Ron sat at the head of the table, next to his queen, Lawanda. And Lord Gerald sat at the end of the table, with his consulting, sitting across the table. Shymair sat next to his mom, Kim, but her husband, General Shummy, and King Ka'Ron's generals were absent.

The land of Galloway was at a time of war. And their plates were served to them by the servants. They ate together and laughed together.

## The next morning

Shymair, Kaiden, and Jessica were outside having fun playing chase tag. "You can't catch me, na-na-na, boo-boo," Jessica said.

"I'm gonna get you," Shymair said.

As they were playing, Lord Gerald watched them play from the window in his bedroom. As he stood by the window, he said to his consulting, "Look at my handsome nephew, joyful, like a flower. Promising with a bright future, heir to the throne. King Kaiden of Lycanthrope. He doesn't even know the truth."

"He is heir to the throne," the consulting said.

Lord Gerald turned around from the window and looked at his consulting and said, "Indeed, he is. But indeed, he might not be. I will reclaim the throne for my pathetic brother, and he will perish under my muddy wet boot!"

"I'm by your side, my lord. Your father should have given you the crown, he made an unwise choice. I see your anger, displeasure."

"My father's choice was taken from him, and I will take it back. But until then, we will move silently, like a lion hunting for his prey. For my brother is that prey, and I am that lion."

"We must plan carefully, my lord."

"Yes, we will play it safe."

## Meantime

In the throne hall, King Ka'Ron was sitting in his royal chair, his wife, Lawanda, sat next to her king, as a proud queen she was. And the king was hearing the voices of the people of the town of Galloway, one voice at a time. There was a farmer complaining about local wolves attacking his flock, and the king said, "I will have my builders build you a strong gate."

"Thank you, my king."

There was another local complaining about her roof leaking water, and she said, "I have no man or handyman around the house, my king. My husband left me and my children years ago."

"I will send someone who is handy, to fix your roof for you and your children."

"Thank you, my king."

"Next!" King Ka'Ron said.

Shummy walked in the throne hall.

"Ahhh, General Shummy, what good news do you bring me?"

"I wish to speak with you privately, my king."

King Ka'Ron stood up and said, "People of Galloway, let's take a brief moment."

King Ka'Ron sat back down and waited for the people to leave the throne hall. When everyone finally left, the king said, "Speak your peace."

General Shummy said, "We have the enemy on the run, we broke through their defenses, they are no match for your military. Soon King Hector the Vampire's land will be yours."

"That is good news, and what of King Hector the Vampire?"

"He fled his castle through one of his secret tunnels. We have our soldiers out looking for him. Your second general, Khalifa, is commanding the search."

"You have done well," King Ka'Ron said proudly.

And then Queen Lawanda said, "Yes, you have done excellently, brother-in-law."

"Thank you both."

"I am proud that you are my general. I shall reward my generals, and my soldiers with extra pay."

"You are kind, my king. But may I request my reward? I speak plainly."

"As you may."

"With your blessing. I wish to have my own werewolf clan and be the leader of my people. As my father was a great leader of his people," General Shummy said.

And then Queen Lawanda said, "You wish to leave us?"

But King Ka'Ron said, "Your father, Lord Maximus, was a great lord. Died in battle as a true werewolf warrior, his name will forever be remembered. What you are requesting from me, it's a hard decision. You are my third general, some of my soldiers and some of the people of Galloway will leave with you, under your command...but it is your birthright."

General Shummy said, "You will always have my loyalty, my king."

"I believe I do. As my brother-in-law and as your birthright, in the name of your father, Lord Maximus. I will grant your request, you will be a lord. But as your king, after the war is won, you have my blessings to begin your journey."

"Thank you, my king."

And then Queen Lawanda said, "No, thank you, for everything you have done."

"May Yeshua be with you. This conversation may end."

## Fourth days later, early in the morning

King Ka'Ron and Prince Kaiden went for a walk through the woods. Birds were chirping, squirrels running and jumping on trees, rabbits hopping about, a fox hunting a raccoon, and the king said to his son, "Son, do you know why I bring you out here?" The king asked Kaiden a rhetorical question.

"No, Father, I do not."

"I brought you out here, my son, because one day, you will be the king of this land. And you must be great to people. Be there for the people, not just for the people. Hear their words, you must be righteous, just, and merciful, for your God, Yeshua, is merciful. You will have some people who will love you, and you will have some that will hate you. Use that love to keep you going and use that hate to keep you motivated. Do you understand, my son?"

"Yes, Father."

"The time will come when your mother and I will choose a queen for you."

"Father, why do you and Mother choose my queen?"

"It's the traditional way of royalty. But remember these: Be a king to the people and be a good husband to your wife. And have the wisdom to know the difference between the two."

"I will try, Father."

They walked deeper into the woods, and King Ka'Ron said, "You're not just out here for a lecture."

"What else, Father?"

The king stopped his son from walking, looked at him, placed his hand on Kaiden's shoulder, and said, "For a good hunt. You see that large male brown bear, about over a hundred fifty yards back on the right?"

"Wow. Good eye, Father, I didn't even notice."

"I've been tracking it since we started this walk. Move quietly and watch."

The king turned into a werewolf and jumped high into the air, landing on a big tree. He moved slow and quietly through the branches, stalking his prey. The brown bear was eating berries, unaware he was being hunted. The king quickly jumped down from the tree, grabbed the bear by the back of its head, lifted the bear's head, and bit the bear's neck, ripping the bear's throat out with his sharp teeth, killing it instantly. The king turned back to normal, the bear's blood pouring down his chest from his mouth. As he wiped the blood off, he told his son to come. When Kaiden approached his father, the king said to him, "Do you see, son? You must be quiet, stealthy, and attack at the appropriate time."

"I see, Father."

"What you kill, you eat, and what you don't eat, you leave for the earth to swallow."

"I understand."

"And never kill a human, unless they are a threat. For we live among them on our land, we protect them."

"When I'm older, I'll be strong and fast like you, Father."

"In due time, my son, when your body is more mature. You're too young to take on the form of a werewolf. But until then, your combat training begins two years from now. You are a skilled fighter, and I am proud of you, my son. For I am proud of you now."

"Thank you, Father."

The king smiled at him and said, "Now pick up the bear and carry it back home so we can feast."

"Yes, sir."

Prince Kaiden picked up the bear and carried it on his shoulder; they walked back to the castle.

## Three weeks had passed

The war was finally over, and King Ka'Ron celebrated victory in the throne hall with his high-ranking three generals and his thirty captains. They were eating, laughing, drinking, raising their wooden tankards, banging their fists on the table, and shouting, "Galloway! Galloway! Galloway! Galloway!"

General Maximus stood up and yelled, "Your king is about to speak! Quiet down!"

He sat back down, and the king stood up and said, "I am proud of each one of you for protecting our family. We are family! And for protecting our children. And for fighting for what is right! I am a very proud alpha king werewolf. Now let us celebrate!" The king sat back down in his royal chair, and his captains yelled, shouted, and cheered, some of them even wrestled.

It's the fourth morning, and King Ka'Ron's brother-in-law, General Shummy, and his people were packing their belongings, preparing for their journey.

Prince Kaiden approached Shymair and said to him, "You're really leaving us, cousin?"

With a sad face, Shymair answered and said, "Yes, my dad said it's time for us to follow our path."

"Where will you go?"

"He said we are heading up north."

Jessica ran toward Shymair with her arms open, and she wrapped her arms around him and gave him a big hug, saying, "I'm going to miss you."

"Okay, okay. I'm going to miss you too. Let me go, will you."

And then Prince Kaiden said, "Make sure you write."

Shymair responded and said, "I barely know how to read. I'm only eight years old."

"You better learn," Jessica said.

Kaiden, Jessica, and Shymair laughed.

"Okay, I will," Shymair said.

Shummy walked toward them and said to his son, Shymair, "Boy, time to go!"

"Yes, father."

Shummy laid his hand on Kaiden's shoulder and said to him, "You will make a fine king one day. Make your father and us were-wolves proud."

Kaiden looked up toward him and said, "I will, sir."

Shymair and Kaiden hugged and said their goodbyes to each other. Shymair and his father walked toward the horse cart where the others were waiting for them. Then King Ka'Ron and Queen Lawanda walked outside the castle with her sister Kim, walking toward the horse cart. When they approached, Kim said to Shummy, "Husband, are we ready to go?"

He looked at her and said, "Yes, let us be on our way."

Kim hugged her nephew Kaiden and said, "You be good."

Kaiden looked up at her and said, "I will, Auntie."

Queen Lawanda walked toward Shummy with her arms open and said, "May your journey be safe."

He hugged her back and said, "Thank you." Then Kim approached Shummy because the time for them to leave was near. He grabbed her by the waist, picked her up, and put her inside the horse carrier. As he was doing so, King Ka'Ron said to him, "I wish you would stay. But I understand a man must follow his own path."

Shummy placed his hand on King Ka'Ron's shoulder, looked at him, and said, "Indeed, a man must." They shook hands and then embraced each other in a hug. Then Shummy said to Shymair, "Time to go, son." He picked him up and put him inside the horse carrier with his mom. Then Shummy climbed up on the horse carrier, looked at them, and said, "Farewell, family." They rode off and waved.

Lord Gerald was looking out the window, watching them leave. "Good riddance," he said in a hateful voice, then he walked away from the window.

## Two years later and three went by

And it's the month of the year for all young boys of the land of Galloway to begin their combat training. They run, jog, do push-ups, sit-ups, learn how to fight with swords and daggers, and hand-to-hand combat training. They also learn how to control their were-wolf transformation. While the young soldiers are in training, Prince Kaiden was learning his combat training with Jackie Lee, who was Kaiden's one-on-one instructor. He thought Kaiden the art of hand-to-hand combat with boxing and mixed martial arts and the way of understanding a sword. Jackie Lee did not take it easy on Kaiden, for a prince's title does not matter here in the temple called the Moon and the Sun. It was a temple that sat on a high mountain in Galloway.

When you step outside of the temple and walk to the edge of the mountain, you look down and see the training camp of the young boys becoming soldiers. Jackie Lee threw big rocks at him, teaching him how to dodge, and when he didn't dodge, he learned the pain. He shot arrows at him. Kaiden knew what would happen if he did not dodge the arrows; he will be hit. Months had gone by in Kaiden's training, and he had gotten better, stronger. Jackie Lee said to Kaiden, "You have done well, my young student, now it's time for a duel."

"Yes, Sensei."

They were both in their fighting stance. Kaiden charged at him, jumped in the air with a flying kick.

Jackie Lee blocked it with his right hand, grabbed Kaiden by the leg, spun him around, and threw him in the air.

Kaiden caught his balance on the wall and jumped off, charging at him like a speeding bullet.

Jackie Lee kicked him with a spin kick.

Kaiden spun in the air like a tornado and hit the floor. As he was getting up off the floor, he said in an angry voice, "I'm not giving up!"

"Control your anger. Do not let your anger control you. You must stay focused. Breathe! Let's try again!"

Kaiden struck with a left, right, left, another left, then right, and a kick.

Jackie Lee blocked the punches and the kick, and he struck back with a right straight punch, a left straight punch, another left straight punch, then a right uppercut, followed up with a left elbow.

Kaiden blocked the punches but was hit with the left elbow, causing him to stumble, but he quickly caught his balance and hit Jackie Lee with a good right punch, almost knocking him off his feet.

He caught himself from falling and stood still, grabbing his chin and rubbing it, and said, "Good, very good, my young student. Now we can move on. But continue practicing always."

"Yes, Sensei."

Three years of Prince Kaiden's training, and he had begun to learn the skills of a sword. Weeks passed, and he learned the skills of a spear.

The next day, Jackie Lee was teaching him how to use a bow and arrows, and he said to Kaiden, "Breathe, take your time, focus. Release!"

Kaiden hit the target and said, "Bull's-eye! I'll shoot it right in the middle." You could hear the excitement in Kaiden's voice, and Jackie Lee said, "Good, good. You're getting better at this."

"I'm getting pretty good."

Then Jessica approached them and said, "Hey, Kaiden, would you like to go for a swim?"

"Ohhh, I'd love to," Kaiden said with excitement.

He looked at Jackie Lee and said, "Can I go, Sensei?"

He answered with a smile and said, "Of course, you can. We can start again tomorrow." Jackie Lee yelled out, "*You two have fun!*"

"Come on!" Jessica said as they were still running.

"Yessss! Thank you, Sensei."

Jessica and Kaiden ran off as they were running.

Kaiden ran behind her, and she said, "Last one there is a rotten egg."

"You know I'm faster than you!"

They laugh and laugh, having the best time of their lives, without a care in the world. Just young children having fun in life. They finally arrived at the lake, Jessica dived in, Kaiden swung from a big vine tree and dropped in.

While they were swimming, Jessica asked, "Do you think we will see Shymair again?"

Kaiden answered, "I don't know. I hope so, it's been over two years now. I'm pretty sure he's doing great."

Jessica floated backward and said, "I hope so. I miss him."

Kaiden floated on his back and said, "Me too. Shymair is my favorite cousin, we are like brothers. And I know where to look for him if I ever need to. I know Uncle Shummy and my dad write each other letters."

Jessica swam out of the lake and said, "Then I shouldn't have any worries then." She grabbed the vine tree, swung off, and cannonballed in, making a big splash. They laughed and swam until their hands turn wrinkly.

### The next day

Kaiden was back at Jackie Lee's training room in the temple of the Moon and the Sun, and he said to Kaiden as they were sitting on the floor cross-legged facing each other, "You must control your anger, for when you finally turn into a lycanthrope, you must have discipline and control your rage. Do not let it control you."

"When do I turn into a lycanthrope?"

"For born werewolves, when the body is ready. I've seen others who were bitten, and they turned on a full moon and have no memory of it, until they were taught how to use it. That's why you must be part of a pack, so the alpha can guide you. For a born werewolf, many full moons can pass, and he or she will not turn until the body is completely ready for the transformation. And born werewolves are connected to the spirits of heaven and nature. Bitten werewolves are not."

"I understand, Sensei."

"Oh, you do? Well then, answer this. Who is stronger? The werewolf who was born or the one who was bitten?"

Kaiden answered, "The one who was born."

"And why?"

"It's through the bloodline, and the older you are, the stronger you become."

Jackie Lee smiled as he was proud to say, "Correct. That is why your father is the king. And tell me of a female werewolf?"

And he answered, "They don't possess the strength like a male. But they possess speed, for their muscles are not like males, so they're faster and good hunters."

"Good, very good. Now tell me your educational of vampires."

"Yes, Sensei. Vampires who were bitten are just normal regular vampires. They have speed and strength, but their strength is no equal to a born werewolf. Bitten vampires are only equal to a bitten werewolf."

And Jackie Lee said, "You have answered correctly. I am proud of you. Now tell me of a born vampire?"

Kaiden answered, "Only a born vampire is blessed with a natural gift of abilities. Each born vampire possesses one of their own abilities. They are very strong and very fast and have eternal life, unlike a born werewolf, who can live up to nearly two thousand years, but born vampires are not connected to the spirits, neither are bitten ones."

"And who becomes king and queen?"

"Born blood royalty of werewolves, vampires, and humans."

"Correct once again. And now for the final question. Where do all lycanthropes and vampires descend from?"

Kaiden answered, "Vlad the Impaler, Dracula. Son of the devil."

"Good, young prince, very good."

Kaiden looked down like he was bothered with something, and Jackie Lee noticed and said, "Why worry oneself?"

Kaiden said with a soft voice, "Sensei, there's something else I would like to talk to you about."

"Look at me," Jackie Lee said with concern in his voice. "What is it? You may speak."

Kaiden looked up toward him and said, "I keep having dreams of an old ancient vampire fighting a werewolf. Having these dreams often. And I believe they are brothers. It always ends with the vampire killing his brother."

Jackie Lee said, "That sounds like the ancient story of Cain and Abel."

With a confused face, Kaiden said, "Dracula's two sons? Why would I have dreams of them?"

"I don't know. Sounds like the prophecy."

Kaiden looked more confused and said, "What prophecy? I didn't study that one."

"The spirit of Abel will vessel himself in his champion. Maybe you are his champion."

Kaiden smirks and said, "I doubt that."

Jackie Lee got up off the floor and said, "If you believe." Then he said, "Now let us begin training."

Kaiden got up and said, "Yes."

Years have passed, and Kaiden was now nineteen years old and had completed his training.

# Chapter 3

# The Primordial Werewolf

At the temple, Kaiden was gathering his things, for he was preparing to leave, for his time has come for him to be done with his training, and Jackie Lee approached him and said, "You have done well, my student. I'm proud to see the young man you have become. Your father will be proud! And remember to always practice."

Kaiden finished packing his bag, put the bag down, looked at Jackie Lee, and said, "Yes, Sensei."

They embraced each other with a hug, then Jackie Lee folded his hands behind him and walked away. Kaiden grabbed his bag and left; he walked his journey off the mountain.

Moments later, he finally returned to the castle. When he arrived at the castle, he yelled out, "*Father, Mother, I am home!*"

The help walked toward him and said, "The king and queen stepped out for a brief moment, my young prince. I believe they are dining with King Richard."

Kaiden asked, "And of my uncle? Where is he?"

She answered, "He's out on business."

"That sounds about right with him. Where is Jessica?"

The help hesitated to answer the question. "Oh, right."

She looked away from him and said, "Her mother had to take a leave of absence from work." She looked back at him and said, "Because Jessica has been very ill, my young prince."

Kaiden began to walk away, heading toward Jessica and her mom's room.

The help said, "No, they're not here in the castle. They have returned home to treat her illness." Then Kaiden turned around toward her and said, "Thank you." He left immediately, rushing to Jessica's house. He took one of the horses, hopped on the horse, and took off like he was in a horse race. Moments later, he finally arrived at Jessica's house, got off the horse, and rushed to her door. He knocked on the door.

Someone inside said, "Yes! Who is it?"

"It is I, Prince Kaiden. I'm here to see Jessica."

"Please, come in."

Kaiden entered the house, and the mother of Jessica looked at him and said, "I'm glad you came, young prince. She's been asking for you. She's in her room. I just gave her some tea, please go see her."

"Yes, ma'am."

He entered the room and saw her lying in bed like death. She looked pale, her eyes were burning red, her nose was red, and she wheezed as she was breathing.

"Oh, dear Yeshua in heaven," Kaiden said as tears rolled down his eyes. She tried to speak with a low voice of wheezing, "Nah, don't come…in here with your sympathy…I need you…to be tough. For I am strong, young prince."

Kaiden grabbed the chair from the corner of the room and sat next to her by the bed, wiped the tears from his eyes, grabbed Jessica's right hand, looked at her, and said, "I will be strong for you."

"How was…your training?" she asked him.

"Let's just say, I can kick your ass with one finger."

She replied with her wheezing, "I'd like…to see you…try." She began to cough, and she tried to speak, then Kaiden said as he gently rubbed her head, "Hey now, take it easy."

She said, "I remember…when we were kids… You couldn't even…beat me in a sword stick fight."

Kaiden continued to rub her head, and as he was still holding her hand, he said, "That was a good match, and I would like a rematch. And how about we go for another swim?"

She tried to say, "How much, I would…love to go for a dip in the lake. And maybe, this time…we can go to see Shymair… Do you think he knows of my…illness?"

Kaiden rested his back against the chair, placed both hands on his lap, and said, "I don't know. I honestly just got back today, and when I heard you were sick, I came here as fast as I could. How long have you not been well?"

She tried to say, "My illness has had a hold of me for about three weeks. And I fear, it's not getting better… The physicians can't figure it out. So they treat me with antibiotics and honey tea… I'm strong."

Kaiden pointed his finger at her and said, "You are strong." Then he reached toward her, gently placed his hand on her cheek, and rubbed it softly, saying, "You will get better soon. You're my best friend, we are in this together." Then he reached over and kissed her on the forehead. He got up, grabbed the chair, placed the chair back in the corner, looked at her, and said, "Now try to get some sleep. I should see you tomorrow."

She looked at him and said, "I love you, big bro."

As he was walking out of the room by her door with his hand on the door handle, he opened the door, looked back at her, and said, "I love you more," and smiled at her. Then left the room and shut the door behind him. Kaiden said goodbye to everyone in the house as he was leaving. He got back on the horse and made his way back to the castle. When he arrived, he went into the kitchen to grab himself something to eat, then went to his room, shut the door, lay on his bed, thought of his friend Jessica, for she was like a sister to him, and cried himself to sleep.

## The next day

Kaiden went to visit Jessica. When he arrived, she was even more sick than before. She could barely speak, so their conversation was very short. After he visited Jessica, he returned to the castle to speak with his father about Jessica's illness. The king was in the throne room speaking with his councils of Galloway. Kaiden entered the room, and when he approached the king, he said, "Father, may I have a word with you?"

The king told his councils, "Gentlemen, let's conclude this meeting." As the king was waiting for his council to leave the throne room, he went to sit in his throne chair. When the king sat down and the councils finally left the room, the king said to Kaiden, "Speak your peace, my son."

Kaiden stood tall and said, "It's about Jessica, Father, She's very ill, and it appears the physician cannot help her."

"What are you proposing?" the king asked.

"Bite her. And she will turn into one of us, and she will be healed. I'm proposing you save her life."

"Out of the question."

"Why? Father, she's dying," Kaiden asked as you could hear the anger in his voice.

"Do not raise your tone of voice to me! Check yourself before you speak. Remember, I'm your father and your king. Now I understand your concern for your friend. So I will answer your question. While you were in training, I was already aware of Jessica's illness. I sent for her mother and offered for her daughter to be like us."

"And?" Kaiden asked, impatient for the answer.

"She refused. For her daughter to be bitten, it's against their godly religion, in the name of the heavenly father, Yeshua. She was born a human, she will die a human. It's their belief, and it's their right."

Kaiden's heart filled with hope, and he said, "There must be something I can do."

"What you can do is respect her mother's wishes."

Kaiden got angry and said, "This is what her mother wishes, not Jessica's!"

The king got frustrated, made a tight fist, hit the edge of his armrest, cracking it, and said, "You will respect her mother's wishes, and there is nothing you can do. And if you even so much as think to overstep your boundaries, punishment will be taking place for your actions."

In anger, Kaiden threw his hands up and said, "Bullshit! Just bullshit! If only I was able to transform, I'd bite her myself."

The king quickly got up and smacked him, saying, "That's twice you have raised your voice to me! You will remain in your room until I say so."

The king yelled out, "Guards! Escort my son to his room, at once!"

The king sat back down in his royal throne chair, and Kaiden looked up at the king and said, "Father!"

"Boy! Say another word, and I'll throw you in the dungeon for a week."

Kaiden remained silent, discouraged, then the guards came to escort him to his room.

Later that night, the king was in his bedroom chamber with his queen. He looked out the window and noticed his brother returning home late with consulting and twelve guards, and the king said, "Where do you always go, brother?"

As the queen was getting into her nightgown, she said, "I heard from the grapevine. You and our son had a little disagreement?"

He turned around from the window, looked at her, and said, "Before I answer your question, I would like to say, you look magnificent in that nightgown. Like a red rose plucked from the garden. You arouse me."

She put both of her hands on her hips and said, "I am flattered, my king. Now, my question to your answer."

"The boy wishes for Jessica to become a werewolf to heal her from the illness. I offered it to Jessica's mother, she refused. And as king, I will not go against her religious beliefs. The boy got upset, he raised his voice. I got a little angry."

The queen said, "A little angry?"

And then the king continued to say, "And I smacked him." The king looked frustrated and said, "Love, I didn't even get a chance to tell him we visited King Richard yesterday, about her son marrying his daughter, Evelyn." The king walked away from the window and toward the bed and sat on the edge of the bed, resting both of his hands on his knees.

The queen said, "I hope our son finds his new soon-to-be bride pleasant."

"I have faith he will. It's tradition, it worked for me and you. I remember our first time, I was scared and troubled. You looked so beautiful as you do now, my love."

The queen walked toward the king as he was sitting on the edge of the bed. She wrapped her arms around his shoulders and said, "I was scared too, but we grew and learned to love each other. And fell in love and had two beautiful daughters, and you raised my son. But you didn't need to smack him."

And then the king said, "Yes, we did, my love, and you're right, I didn't have to smack him, but he raised my anger." The king wrapped his arms around his wife, and the queen said as she gently rubbed her head through his hair, "I understand, my love, but one thing I do know. Kaiden loves you, and he wishes you to save his friend."

And then the king looked up at her and said, "Kaiden wishes to go against Jessica's mother's wishes. And bite her himself and ignoring their religious beliefs." Then the king looked down and said, "But he himself hasn't even transformed yet. I question, what is holding him back? I wonder, is it because he is…"

Before the king had a chance to finish his sentence, Queen Lawanda quickly covered his mouth with one of her fingers and said, "Silent, my husband."

The king looked up at her, got up off the edge of the bed, pulled her closer, engaged into her eyes, and said, "I love you, my queen."

"I love you, my king. But make this right with your son. You are his father, before you are his king."

The king grabbed her butt and squeezed it and said, "You are right, my love, and I will."

They kissed deeply, and he removed her nightgown from her and laid her down in bed.

*Three days had passed*

Zy'Asiah knocked on Kaiden's bedroom door.

"Who is it?" he asked.

"It is I, Zy."

"You may come in."

She entered the room and saw Kaiden sitting on the edge of the bed, watching the mother bird in the tree feeding her baby birds, and he said to her, "What brings you to me, big sis? Is it lunchtime?"

She answered, "No, brother. Father sent me to tell you that you are released from your room."

Kaiden turned his head and looked at her and said, "Oh, did he now?" He said it with a smirk.

"Adrianna told me she overheard you and father arguing. She told Mother too and had her swear it didn't come from her. So please, don't say anything about what I just told you. And I'm just curious, are you still angry with him?"

Kaiden turned his head back around and continued to look out the window to watch the mother bird feed her baby birds, and he said, "I won't say a word, and no. He's my father, staying angry doesn't help. It's toxic energy."

She smiled and said, "Well, in that case, I'm glad everything's okay."

Kaiden asked her, "Have you heard any news from Jessica?"

"Oh, you should go by her house and speak with her mother. You should hear it from her."

Then Kaiden looked at her and asked, "Why does your voice sound troubled when I ask you of Jessica?"

"Little brother, you should really speak with her mother."

Kaiden got up off the edge of the bed, walked past Zy'Asiah, and left the room. He left the castle, grabbed one of the horses, and got on, heading toward Jessica's house. He rode as fast as possible. Upon finally arriving at her house, he jumped off the horse, approached the door, and knocked.

One of her family members opened the door and said, "Oh, Prince Kaiden. How may I help you?"

"I'm here to speak with Jessica and her mother."

Jessica's mother looked and noticed that it was Kaiden at the door and said, "Let him in, he is a friend of Jessica's."

The family member opened the door and said, "Sorry, my prince."

When he entered the house, he saw Jessica's whole family crying in the living room and in the kitchen; they were all crying and weeping. Kaiden asked the mother, "Is Jessica okay?"

The mother pulled herself together from her tears and said, "My young prince. No, she didn't make it through her illness. She passed away yesterday. She's in heaven with Yeshua now."

Kaiden, feeling sorrowful, said in an emotional voice, "What! No. Impossible!" A teardrop formed in Kaiden's eyes.

Kaiden, in disbelief, rushed to her room, hoping to see Jessica lying in bed, burst open her bedroom door, but saw the bed empty and said, "Oh no." He cried and yelled out, "Noooo!" He left her bedroom, heading toward the front door.

As he was leaving, emotionally upset, Jessica's mother saw him leaving in a hurry, tried to quickly approach him, and said, "Wait, wait. Please wait." She had a letter in her hand that Jessica wrote to him. But Kaiden, so upset, ignored her. He continued to walk out of the house. Kaiden, in so much pain from the death of Jessica, felt something happening to his body. He screamed in agony; his body began to change.

The mother saw Kaiden changing and losing control, and she told one of her family members, "Quick, lock and barricade the door!"

Then Kaiden began to scream in more agony, steam coming from his body as he was ripping his clothes off. Then Jessica's mother said, "I'll go get King Ka'Ron!" She ran to a horse and rode off. And then Kaiden quickly started to run, turning into a werewolf form no one had ever seen before. His eyes turned dark brown, his skin color turned dark brown, but no hair grew on his body, except for the hair on his head in a spiky black hairstyle and facial side hair. His muscles were big and brawny, beefy, built, stacked, burly, hulking, robust. His height was six-foot-seven, his two canine teeth sharp and pointy as a knife, his canine teeth even quivered when a threat was near. He could smell from miles away; his sense of smell gave him the direction of where the threat was coming from. His ears were pointy; he could hear from miles away. His hand claws were so sharp, they could cut through hard steel. His face did not change into an ordinary werewolf; his face was more muscular. His legs were original werewolf digitigrade; he could run a mile within five seconds, and he ran for thirty-six miles in three minutes. Kaiden, unaware that he possessed abilities, was the first of his kind, the first primordial werewolf. Kaiden ran until nightfall, the moon was half-full, and he ran by a nearby lake and rested.

He spotted a bunny hopping, and he quickly grabbed it and ate it. Then he smelled something foul in the air, and his two sharp teeth quivered for a threat is near. He looked and spotted where the foul smell was coming from. Kaiden spotted three muggers hiding in the tree and a group of a family of five, traveling on the road in a horse wagon. The robbers jumped out of the tree, attacking the traveling family.

Kaiden instantly intervened. The first mugger, he punched so hard, he flew twenty-five feet, rolling like ball down a hill and impacting into a tree. Then Kaiden disappeared like a ghost in the wind. The traveling family was trembling and scared, and the two remaining robbers were afraid. The third mugger asked the second one, "Where did he go?" as they both were looking around for the unknown mysterious monster, and the second one answered as he was terrified, "Motherfucker! I don't know!"

The third was shaking and scared to death, and he said, "I never seen anything like that before. Doesn't even look like a damn werew—"

In the blink of an eye, Kaiden grabbed him before he even had a chance to finish his sentence and ripped his head off.

The last mugger standing was shocked and said, "Oh, shit! I'm getting the hell out of here!" But before the last mugger even had a chance to flee, Kaiden threw the other mugger's head at him, causing the mugger to stumble and fall. As he was on the ground trying to get up, Kaiden approached him fast like the drop of a water. Before the mugger even had to chance to get up, Kaiden picked him up.

"Oh, no, no, no!" was his last words before Kaiden punched hole through his heart. The first mugger Kaiden punched into a tree was waking up from being unconscious; he could barely get up because a few of his bones are broken. Kaiden approaches him slowly; the mugger was covered in blood with his bones. He was on his knees, and as he saw the monster slowly coming toward him, as Kaiden was approaching him, and the mugger said, "Please, show mercy."

Kaiden ignored his plea and picked him up and bit him on the neck, ripped out his throat, and threw his body. Kaiden was covered in the mugger's blood. Then he slowly approached the traveling family; they were scared and terrified, and the husband said, "Please, we don't want any trouble, now."

Then the wife said, "We're grateful for your help."

But Kaiden was not in control; the werewolf transformation was too powerful for him to control, for he is the first primordial werewolf. He didn't realize what he was doing. His mind was a simple, mindless beast, unaware of his actions. Kaiden continued to approach them slowly, and he flexed both of his hands open, his pointy fingernails were razor-sharp, his intentions were to kill them like a mass murderer. The kids in the back of the horse wagon were holding each other, crying.

One of the children said, "Yeshua, please protect us."

Then the husband said as he quickly grabbed a shovel from the back of the horse wagon, "Please, don't hurt my family!"

Kaiden heard nothing, and he continued to growl at the mouth, like a rabid dog. But then, Kaiden saw a little girl in the back of the horse wagon carrier, terrified as she was holding her two younger brothers. Kaiden's senses kicked in because the little girl reminded him of Jessica. He slowly backed up from the family, then looked and saw five werewolf soldiers quickly approaching him. He growled and took off. They chase after him, but Kaiden was so fast, they couldn't keep up with him. They lost him in the chase; they sniffed for his scent, but can't get a trail of Kaiden's scent, for he has no smell. He was hiding above them in a tree. He quietly jumped down from the tree behind them and landed without making a sound, grabbed one of them from behind, and jumped back up into the tree with the one he grabbed. The other four werewolves didn't even notice yet that one of them was missing. The werewolf Kaiden grabs, he killed him in the tree and dropped him in front of them. They looked up to see where he dropped from, but then Kaiden jumped down from the tree, and grabbed the second werewolf soldier by the mouth and ripped his jaw out. Then he picked up his headless body and threw the headless werewolf body at the third werewolf soldier so hard, he flew through trees, stumbling and rolling with his dead friend werewolf soldier next to him. He was knocked out unconscious and turned back to normal. Then the fourth and the fifth werewolf soldiers charged at Kaiden, trying to wrestle him to the ground. But Kaiden flip, twisted high in the air over them, and landed behind them, smashing their heads together, like two watermelons. The third werewolf soldier was waking up from being unconscious, stumbling to get up. Kaiden saw him getting up and quickly approached him.

As he saw Kaiden approaching him in a rage, he rushed to say to him, "Prince Kaiden, please! Your father sent—" But Kaiden heard nothing he said, and before he even had a chance to speak his words, Kaiden grabbed him by face and picked him up. He tried to speak but was unable to, "My prince, please."

Kaiden crushed his head like a crushed apple.

Afterward, Kaiden ran off and ran for miles and miles through the night of bright stars shining upon him. He tired himself out and came across a wooden house with a family sleeping inside. He dared not bother them, for he was too tired to even bother them. He looked and noticed they have a watering trough for the horses. He licked his lips, for he was thirsty, and dragged his feet across the grass to get a drink of water. As he was drinking the water, he stopped for a second because he saw a reflection in the water that was not his reflection. He did not recognize the reflection in the water; it was Abel. Then Kaiden passed out from being exhausted from running all night. He laid right next to the watering trough, fell into a very deep sleep in a trance, having a vision, and then his body turned back to normal. In the vision, he saw a bright light tunnel, like the gates of heaven, and saw a woman walking toward him, and when the woman approached him, she said, "My son has chosen you."

"Chosen me?" he asked, looking confused.

And the woman said, "Do you know the story of Cain and Abel?"

"Yes, the sons of Adam. Cain killed Abel."

With a smile, she said, "I am Cain and Abel's mother, my name is Cleo. Yeshua has blessed me to be the spirit mother of guidance. My son Abel has chosen for his spirit to live on in you as one. You will have his strength, his speed, and his knowledge. You will be unstoppable, you have no equal. You are the primordial werewolf, the powerful one. This is a gift but a curse to his brother, Cain."

"I'm grateful, but why me?"

"Abel watched you take your first breath and felt the spirit of your pure heart."

"But I almost killed a family."

"Yes. You had no control of your actions. You knew in your heart it was wrong, you stepped back because you know that is not who you are. You must control this gift, especially for what is to come."

Kaiden looked confused and asked, "What is coming?"

Then Kaiden woke up from his vision, got up off the floor, looked around, and realized he was in an underground dungeon cell. He said to himself, "How the hell did I get in here?" He heard someone walking down the stairs but can't see who and said, "I believe there's been a mistake! My father is King Ka'Ron." The unknown person finally approached Kaiden's cell and said, "Using your blood royalty to get yourself out of jail, little brother?"

"My big sister, I'm so glad to see you, Adrianna," Kaiden said, happy to see her. Then he asked her, "What the hell am I doing in here?"

Adrianna answered, "Well, this is father's dungeon. You wouldn't know, it's not like you come down here to visit anyone. But the reason why you're in here is for your safety and for everyone else's."

Kaiden, confused, clutched his hands on the cell bars and asked, "What do you mean for everyone's safety?" Kaiden, sad, shook his head, looked down with a low voice, and said, "I am not a threat."

She walked closer to his cell to grab his hands on the cell bars and said, "I believe you, little brother. But this is father's order."

He looked back up with watery eyes, looked into her eyes, and said, "I don't understand, sis."

And then she said, "When you transformed for the first time, it was a form no one has ever seen before. The people of Galloway say it's the legendary form of Abel, the primordial werewolf. Wolf man."

Kaiden stepped back from the cell bars and said, "Wolf man?"

Adrianna stepped back from his cell bars and said, "Yes. The traveling family are the witnesses. They said you saved them from the muggers. You killed those sneak thieves, but before that, when you left Jessica's house, her mother rushed to go tell our father you needed help. Father sent five werewolf soldiers for you, to bring you home, but you killed them. It's impossible how you did it. Father is worried for you."

Kaiden sat on the bed, looked at her, and said, "Sister, I have little memory of this, it feels like a blur." As Kaiden sat on the bed, he rest his back against the wall, looked straight ahead, and then said, "But I do remember a woman, like in a spiritual vision."

"A woman?" Adrianna asked.

"She spoke to me." Then Kaiden looked at her and said, "Yeah. But just forget it, it's not important. Let's focus on the here and now. When am I getting out of here?"

"Our father is afraid for you, he worries deeply. When he is ready, he will speak with you. But until then, you will remain here for precaution."

As Kaiden began to lay down on the bed, he said, "I have no choice," and then he crossed his legs, folded his fingers behind his head, and said, "I'll just take a nice long nap."

And she said, "Well then, brother, see you soon. I'll have the guards bring you something to eat."

"Thank you, big sister."

"I will leave you now."

Adrianna left the cell dungeon, and the guard brought Kaiden's food. Before the guard got closer to his cell, Kaiden said, "Guard! Give this portion of my food to the other prisoners. I will not be rude and eat well in their faces."

The guard said, "As you wish."

Each prisoner said, "Thank you, Prince."

"Thank you!"

"Thank you, my Prince."

"The time will come when you make a great king."

Then Kaiden said, "Blessed be you all, in the name of Yeshua." He made himself more comfortable in the bed, fluffing the pillow, and saying, "Good night." And he rested until tomorrow.

# Chapter 4

# Lord Gerald

*Two weeks before*

The day was night, the moon was orange bright, the stars were shining, and Lord Gerald was on the road traveling to speak with a vampire king named King Philip in a land called Cumberland. Traveling with him was his consulting; they were traveling in a royal horse carriage, sitting comfortably inside, with six werewolf soldiers on their horses, riding in front of them. Riding behind, them are six more werewolf soldiers. Lord Gerald said to his traveling companions as they were about to enter the land of Cumberland, "We are about to enter the land of vampires. Everyone, keep your cool. They know of our arrival."

The consulting was concerned and said, "I hope they show great hospitality. Vampires are snooty creatures who look down on us as dogs."

Lord Gerald, looking out the window enjoying the view of his travels, said, "When we ride inside, they shall look at us as dogs." Then Lord Gerald looked at his consulting and said, "But when we ride out, they shall look at us as equal allies."

"I hope you're right, my lord."

They finally enter the land of Cumberland, and the vampires of the land looked at them with dirty looks as they ride through. The servants of the vampires, who were familiars—humans who wished to be vampires—some of them spit as they were riding by. A few of the vampires were whispering to one another as they watched them ride through their land, saying, "What are those filthy dogs doing here?"

"They reek of dog shit."

"They smell like wet dogs."

One familiar said, "Filthy animals," and then he spit.

They continued to ride through. When they arrived near the gates of the castle, five vampire soldiers approached them, and one of the vampire soldiers said, "What is your business here?"

Lord Gerald opened the royal horse carriage door, got out, looked at the soldier, and said, "I am Lord Gerald. I have an audience with King Philip. Here is my letter from the king, signed by the king." He handed the letter over to the soldier.

He read the letter and then handed Lord Gerald back his letter and said, "Open the gate! Let them pass!"

Lord Gerald got back inside the horse carriage, shut the door behind him, and said to his consulting, "I told you we'd be all right."

"I never doubted you, my lord."

They rode through the gate and arrive at the castle. Lord Gerald and his consulting both get out of the royal horse carriage. The consulting grabbed a big box off the royal horse carriage and carried the big box, and they followed behind the soldier to announce their arrival to the king. The twelve werewolf soldiers stayed by the royal horse carriage. They arrived at the throne room, and the vampire soldier opened both doors, walked inside, and said to the king, "My king! Lord Gerald and his consulting are here for your audience."

King Philip got up and greeted them with a handshake, saying, "Lord Gerald. How was the travel?"

The vampire soldier left the throne room, and Lord Gerald said to the king, "Quite relaxing, King Philip."

"Did any of my people give you a hard time?"

Being sarcastic, he answered, "Oh, no. They were very…lovely bloodsuckers."

King Philip placed his hand on Lord Gerald's right shoulder and said, "Your words are too kind, Lord Gerald." Then King Philip removed his hand off Lord Gerald's shoulder, folded his hands together, and said, "Both of you are just in time for dinner. Please, follow me to the dining room."

They followed the king toward the dining room, and the consulting quietly whispered in Lord Gerald's ear, saying, "I heard a rumor that vampires have human blood in their food."

Lord Gerald whispered back, saying, "We shall soon find out."

One of the families who was the help of the castle opened the dining room door. When they entered inside the dining room, Lord Gerald saw two women already sitting by the dinner table. When they approached the two women, they stood up from the dinner table, and Lord Gerald said to the king, "Well, I assume these two lovely ladies are your wife and daughter?"

And King Philip looked at Lord Gerald and said, "Yes. This is my wife, Helen, the Queen of Cumberland."

Lord Gerald shook Helen's hand and said to her, "It's a pleasure to meet you."

With a smile, she said, "Oh, the pleasure is mine."

Then King Philip said so proudly, "And my daughter, Princess Ariel, the general of my army."

Princess Ariel shook Lord Gerald's hand and said, "Nice to meet you."

"You as well," he replied. After they shook hands, Lord Gerald looked at King Philip and said, "Your daughter is your general? How precarious." Then Lord Gerald looked at Princess Ariel and said, "You must be an expert in combat."

"Yes, I am. But why precarious?" Princess Ariel asked, curious, and then she said to him, "Is it because it's unlikely for a woman to be a combat general?"

Lord Gerald looked her in the eyes and said, "No, not at all. I find it quite imaginative when a little girl plays soldier."

Princess Ariel got upset and said, "Little girl!" She was ready to punch him in the face but held herself back out of respect for her father.

King Philip said, "Well, that's enough of that now. Honey, Ariel, Lord Gerald and his consulting will be dining with us tonight."

"Oh, how lovely," Queen Helen said.

"Yeah, how lovely," Ariel said with sarcasm. Helen and Ariel sat back down. Then the help pulled out their chairs for them to sit.

King Philip looked at Lord Gerald and whispered close to him, "Please. Keep your insults to yourself."

Then the king looked at Lord Gerald and his consulting and said, "Now let us sit, eat, and discuss business." The three of them sat down, and the servants brought the platter of food out from the kitchen.

"Please, I hope you enjoy the food. And no, there's no human blood in it." When King Philip said those words, the consulting was stuck with a dumb look on his face; he was speechless.

Then the king said, "Lord Gerald." The king looked at him and said, "I was intrigued by the letter you sent me. It piqued my interest."

As Lord Gerald was about to eat, he said, "I was concerned that you weren't going to write back. But I was confident you would."

"I see, in your letter. Do you have what you are offering?"

Lord Gerald snapped his fingers to his consulting, telling him, "Bring the box." The consulting handed him the box, and Lord Gerald gave the box to King Philip. He said to him as King Philip opened the box, "Ten hundred gold bars and twenty thousand pieces of silver, for our agreement."

As King Philip looked at the shining gold bars, he said, "Lord Gerald. You are a werewolf of your word."

Then Lord Gerald said with passion, "If I didn't have my word, I would have nothing."

The king looked back up and said, "Well then. I'll keep up my end of the bargain." King Philip rested his back against the chair, grabbed his cup of blood wine, drank it, put it back down, and looked at Lord Gerald and said, "I'll help you kill your brother. Stage a fake war, he dies in battle. Long live the king! You take the throne."

"The throne has always been rightfully mine."

"I have no concern with what is rightfully yours. I'm getting paid, and you will continue to pay me. But what does concern me is your nephew. He is next in line to rule, is he not?"

"Have no concern with my nephew, I am taking care of that. And what of that someone who has a particular skill of killing some-one without being detected and nothing will trace back to you?"

"The assassin?"

"Yes. You mentioned in the letter."

"Oh, yes. He works alone and quietly."

"How can I find him?" Lord Gerald asked.

"In the land of Salem. It's about one hour away from here, heading east. Stay on the path of Landis av. When you arrive, look for an oak tree by the lake. It's the only oak tree by the lake. Write a detailed letter of what you need him to do. Roll the letter up and tie it to a bag of a thousand pieces of silver, and place the bag and letter in the hole of the oak tree."

"Then what?" Lord Gerald asked.

"He will contact you."

"Well then."

"Now let us eat."

## The next day

Lord Gerald, the consulting, and the werewolf soldiers left King Philip's land of Cumberland and traveled to Vineland. On their way, the consulting asked, "My lord, how many days shall we stay in Salem? Should I find us a place to accommodate us?"

Lord Gerald looked at him and said, "Yes. Three days shall be fine." Then Lord Gerald looked out the window and said, "We don't want to stay there any longer than we must. Then we shall travel back home."

When they arrived, the consulting departed from them to find them a place to stay for a few nights. Moments later, the consulting returned to tell Lord Gerald he had found them a place to lay their heads for a few days. After they settled in for the night, Lord Gerald wrote the letter.

## The next morning

Lord Gerald went by the lake and placed the letter in the hole of the oak tree with a bag of a thousand pieces of silver tied to it. Later that night, Lord Gerald's werewolf soldiers were on guard; two of them stood outside by the door, and the other ten watched the premises. While he was sitting at the table eating his meal, suddenly, from behind, he felt a sharp dagger near his neck and a crossbow aimed at the back of his head. He dared not move. The assassin said to him in a very quiet voice, "Put your hands on the table slowly."

Lord Gerald slowly put his spoon down and placed both of his hands on the table. The assassin said in a low, quiet voice, "I have received your letter."

Lord Gerald's voice trembled with fear, and he said, "I didn't hear you coming. You got past my guards. Are they alive?"

"Yes," the assassin answered softly.

"You are good. And of my consulting?"

"I knocked him out cold, sleeping like a baby."

"May I turn around to see the man I hired and know his name?"

"No face, no name."

"Being discreet."

"Precisely. I require fifty bricks of gold. I get paid when the job is done. You already paid up front by writing the letter."

"No problem," Lord Gerald said.

"When the job is done, leave the gold in the tree."

"Will do."

The assassin slowly holstered his crossbow and removed the dagger from Lord Gerald's neck. And then the assassin disappeared into the shadows. Lord Gerald finally took a breath.

## The next day

The sun came up, and they gathered their things and prepared for the trip on the road, heading back home. During their travels, the consulting asked Lord Gerald, "Did you handle what you needed to handle?"

He looked at him and said, "Yes. Everything went according to plan."

The consulting smiled proudly and said, "Soon, you shall be king, my lord."

"Indeed."

Later, nightfall came, and they finally returned to the castle. On the night when King Ka'Ron was in his bedroom chamber with his queen, he looked out the window and noticed his brother returning home late with his consulting and twelve werewolf soldiers. The king asked, "Where do you always go, brother?"

# Chapter 5

# Love and War

*Present time*

Early in the morning, King Ka'Ron sent one of his guards to release Kaiden from his cell. When the guard arrived in the dungeon and approached Kaiden's cell door, the guard opened the cell door and said, "Prince Kaiden!" He was in a deep sleep, and he did not hear his name being called. The guard yelled out his name again, "Prince Kaiden! Get up!"

He woke up with a morning face and said, "Yeah, yeah. I'm up, I'm up. Shit."

He got up and sat on the bed, rubbing his eyes, and the guard said, "Your father wishes to speak with you."

Kaiden got up off the bed, and the guard said, "But the king recommends you bathe first and then have breakfast."

Kaiden sniffed his armpit and said, "A bath does sound nice." He walked out of the cell, and the guard closed the cell door behind him. As Kaiden was leaving, one of the prisoners said, "Thank you again for the food you have been giving me. You will make a fine king."

Before Kaiden walked up the steps, he turned around and said, "The pleasure is mine." Then he turned back around and walked up the steps. Kaiden left the dungeon and headed toward the tub room. When he arrived at the tub room, he saw two helper assistants standing by the door with their hands folded by their waists. When

49

he approached, one of the help said, "Everything is ready for you, my prince."

He looked at them and said, "Thank you."

And then one of the help said, "Your meal will be ready for you after your bath, and a fresh pair of clothes is laid out for you on the chair by the tub."

The help opened the door, Kaiden walked into the tub room, and saw the fresh pair of clothes and the lovely bubble bath. He looked back at the help and said, "You ladies are the best."

They smiled and shut the door and walked off. Kaiden lay in the tub, blowing soap bubbles.

Moments later, as he was enjoying his bubble bath, his mind drifted off into deep thought of his friend Jessica. *Wow, she's really gone*, he thought to himself. He tried not to weep and remembered to be strong for her. *The pain still hurts*, he thought to himself. His mind wandered off even more. *I'm curious about what my father wishes to speak with me about. I guess I'll find out after breakfast. I'm hungry.* Kaiden finished soaking his body, got out of the tub, dried off, and put on a fresh pair of clothes. He left the tub room and headed toward the dining room.

When he arrived in the dining room, he sat down at the table, and the servant served him his hot meal. The servant said to him, "Your father told me to inform you. When you are done eating, he will be waiting for you in the garden."

"Thank you, I will."

When he was done eating, the servant came and grabbed his plate. Kaiden got up from the table and looked at the servant and said, "Tell the chef the food was excellent."

She nodded her head and said, "Will do"

Then Kaiden left the dining room and headed toward the garden. When he arrived, he saw his father in the garden, sitting on a stone chair. Kaiden approached him and said, "Father?"

King Ka'Ron got up and looked at his son and said in a calm voice, "I have two horses over there. Grab the horse on the right, and follow me, son."

They walked toward the two horses and got on. The king said, "Let's ride out, son."

Kaiden thought to himself, *Where are we going to?*

Moments later, their horse-riding journey came to an end when they finally arrived at a very big hill. The king got off his horse and said, "Come!" Kaiden got off his horse, and the king said, "Tie the horse here, and walk up with me."

"Yes, Father."

They walked up the hill following the path, and they finally made it to the top of the hill. When they reached the summit, King Ka'Ron said to his son, Prince Kaiden, "Look, son. Look at the land of Galloway."

Kaiden looked at the land and saw families, kids playing outside, farmers growing crops, animals, birds, guards patrolling the land, a shoemaker, a draper, milliners, haberdashers, bakers, butchers, grocers, fishmongers, booksellers. He also saw mountains behind the land of Galloway, and on top of those mountains was Jackie Lee's training temple.

Kaiden looked at his father and said, "It's beautiful."

"When I was a boy," the king said, then he looked at the land and continued, "my father took me to this very same spot." He reached his hand out toward Galloway and said, "He showed me the land of the kingdom of Galloway." Then the king put his hand down and looked at his son, saying, "And told me this will all be yours when it's time for you to reign, and you'll help the people of the community, and they will love you, and they will hate you."

Kaiden asked his father, "Why would some of them hate me?"

The king answered, "Not everyone will always agree with your decisions. It's not always simple being the king. Sometimes you must make tough, rational decisions and sacrifices for what you believe is for the greater good. Do you understand?"

"Yes."

"I believe you will understand better when you are king. As your father, it's my duty to show you the right path and for you to remember my teachings."

Kaiden said with great passion, "I have always heeded your words of wisdom, like a baby elephant following its mother."

Then the king placed his hand on Kaiden's shoulder and looked at him deeply, saying, "Do you respect my decision for you to marry King Richard's daughter and unite the two kingdoms?"

"Is she pretty?"

The king removed his hand from Kaiden's shoulder and asked, "Is that your concern?"

"Would you marry an ugly girl?"

The king tried not to laugh and said, "I will learn to love her. Did you think your mother was ugly at first? Absolutely not! My heart melted the first time my eyes laid upon her. She was beautiful then as she is beautiful now. She is the dove in my eye, the queen of my heaven. I would kill for her and die for her."

Kaiden said, "Then I will do the same."

The king then said with a sad voice, "I'm very sorry for the loss of your friend. My heart goes out to you."

"It's all right, Father. You don't have to say a word. You were doing your duty as king."

"I like I said, son, tough decisions. But the emotion caused by her death led you to turn into the legendary form of Abel. It appears he has chosen you. You are stronger than most, no equal. Your name will ring out through many kingdoms. But you must learn how to control it, for we are at a terrible time."

Kaiden asked, "What do you speak of, Father?"

"We are at war, son. Your uncle informed me. King Philip wishes to attack us for our land and for us to submit under his sword. You are our only hope. With your power and strength, we can win. And when the war is won, we can focus on your wedding. King Richard wishes for his daughter not to be a bride until the war is over."

Kaiden looked at his father with pride and said, "I will bring us to victory, Father."

"Then you will be my number 1 general. You have the power to command my army. Peace comes with war, and war comes with peace."

"Yes, Father."

"Now let us return to the castle and prepare for war."

They walked down from the mountain and returned to their horses. Kaiden said, "I have to go back to Jackie Lee's temple to learn how to control."

"Good, you should go."

They rode off their separate ways, and then Kaiden finally made it to the temple. He entered inside, and Jackie Lee said, "You have finally returned, Prince Kaiden. Are you ready?"

"Yes."

"Then let us begin."

## A week had passed

The day was night, and the moon was full and bright. They are now on the battlefield, with King Ka'Ron's werewolf soldiers and King Philip's vampire soldiers lining up across the field. Kaiden looked at his men and said, *"Are you ready to fight and die for your king?"*

King Ka'Ron was on his horse, watching his son proudly. The king's generals said to Prince Kaiden, "We follow you into victory!" Lord Gerald and his consulting were on their horses, watching from the far left of the battlefield.

King Philip gave his daughter the command for his generals to attack. She raised her sword high in the sky. Then Prince Kaiden gave the command to attack, yelling, *"Charge!"* The soldiers ran toward the enemy, transforming into werewolves. King Philip's archers raised their bows and arrows, and his daughter aimed her sword forward. The generals saw the signal and yelled, *"Fire!"* Hundreds of arrows flew in the sky. Kaiden ran behind his men, transforming as he passed them. He jumped high in the air and thunderclapped, knocking the arrows out of the sky.

Lord Gerald was in shock at what he just witnessed and said, "What the heck!"

Then Kaiden landed back on the ground, and the consulting said, "How extraordinary. I've never seen such power."

King Philip realized that shooting arrows was useless. He told his daughter to order his generals to prepare for combat. She gave the generals the signal, and he yelled, "Kill them all!"

The front line charged into battle, clashing with each other. Vampire soldiers swung their swords, and the werewolf soldiers struck, bit, and ripped apart the vampire soldiers. Blood and guts flew everywhere, covering the battlefield. A vampire soldier swung his sword at Kaiden, but he dipped the swing, grabbed the sword, and used it to chop off the vampire's head before throwing the sword at another vampire soldier. Another one struck at him but missed. Kaiden grabbed him by the arm, ripped his arm off, and used it to strike him so hard that it twisted around. Kaiden moved so fast through the battlefield that no werewolf or vampire saw him coming. His claws sliced through the vampire soldiers, their bodies dropping and burning in seconds.

Meanwhile, as the vampires and werewolves were killing each other, a hired assassin was hiding in a tree about two hundred yards from the battlefield. No one saw him, and Lord Gerald didn't even see him, but he knew he was out there. The assassin had a handmade craft crossbow that could shoot over five hundred yards. He aimed his shot at King Ka'Ron, controlled his breathing to steady his aim perfectly, and had the king in his line of shot. He held his breath and took the shot.

Kaiden heard the whistle of a flying arrow and saw it heading toward his father. He ran so fast that he caught the arrow just in the nick of time before it hit his father. Kaiden turned back to normal and said, "Father! Get out of here. Now!" He ordered the generals, "Go with my father! Protect him!" and ordered some of the werewolf soldiers to follow them.

Lord Gerald was furious and said, "Damn! Just damn!"

The consulting said, "How can he be that fast?"

Lord Gerald and his consulting left the battlefield immediately, as did the assassin. King Philip told his daughter, "I shall return to the castle. Take charge here."

"As you wish, Father."

King Philip left the battlefield, and Princess Ariel ordered the rest of the vampire soldiers to charge into battle. She followed behind her soldiers, riding her horse, swinging her sword, killing as many as she could. She was knocked off her horse and overwhelmed, deeply wounded, and knocked out unconscious.

Hours later, the battle was over, and King Ka'Ron's werewolf soldiers had won the battle. "*Victory is ours!*" they shouted. They walked the battlefield, killing any vampire soldiers lying on the ground who were still alive. They stabbed each one of them, and they burned, turning into ash.

Prince Kaiden came across Princess Ariel unconscious, as she was lying on the ground wounded badly. She was covered in blood, her wounds were cut deeply by werewolf's claws, unable to heal. Kaiden aimed the sword at her heart, but when he looked at her, he saw the face of Jessica, the friend he lost. He couldn't do it; he was unable to drive that sword through her heart. He looked around to see if anyone would notice if he picked her up; no one was paying attention. He saw an opportunity to grab her, so he lifted her up. She tried to say with a low voice, "Put me down," then she passed out. Prince Kaiden carried her off the battlefield, strapping her to the back of his horse and rode off to an abandoned cabin. When he arrived, he picked her up off the back of the horse and carried her inside. She was still unconscious. He laid her on the bed and then he went to the hearth to start a fire. He placed the sword on top of the fireplace mantel and attended to her wounds. Afterward, he sat in the corner, watching her until he fell asleep.

The next day, she was awake but barely.

"Please, I'm not here to hurt you. Try not to move," Kaiden said.

She could barely speak but tried with a low voice, "I need fresh human blood."

Kaiden thought about those three muggers he killed and thought to himself, *I don't think I can do that again.* Kaiden looked at her and said, "I will see what I can do." He left the cabin and hunted.

Later that day, he came back with a dead deer and said to her, "Blood for you and the meat for me." He drained the deer's blood into a bucket and scooped it out into a cup, elevating her head for her to drink. Her wounds slowly healed, but it still wasn't enough, and he said to her, "We can try again soon."

She fell back to sleep, and Kaiden cooked the deer meat. After he ate, he sat back in his corner, watching the fire until he fell asleep.

Later that night, back in the kingdom of Galloway, Lord Gerald was in his room, upset, pacing back and forth, saying to his consulting, "I don't understand what the hell happened." The consulting said, "It appears that your nephew possesses the power of the legendary Abel."

Lord Gerald looked at him and said, "I thought that was a myth, a story for kids." Then suddenly, the consulting was shot in the neck with a needle from a blowpipe. He removed the needle from his neck, looked at it, but his vision was blurry. He tried to say, "Is that a—" but he felt drowsy and passed out before he could even finish his sentence.

The assassin appeared in the shadow and whispered, "Who was the one who caught my arrow?"

"That was my nephew, Prince Kaiden."

"No one is that fast. In your letter, it's written your nephew was unable to turn."

"That is true, but it appears things have changed."

"Things changing compromise my mission. If my mission is compromised, I raise my price."

"The money is no object."

"I can kill your king now if you like."

"No, just lay low. It's too risky, the guards are tight."

"Then you shall hear from me." The assassin disappeared into the shadows.

## The next day

Kaiden continued to give her deer's blood, and her wounds were healing, but still slowly. She said with a low voice, "Why are you helping me? I am your enemy. Without a thought, I would cut your throat."

He looked at her and said, "I believe you would, my lady."

"So why?"

He sat by the fire and said, "You remind me of someone who was very close to me, someone I could not save. I tried, but I failed."

"Who?" Princess Ariel asked.

"It doesn't matter who, they're gone now. But I promise you this, I swear to you, I'm not here to hurt you or kill you, even though we are enemies. When your wounds are completely healed, and you are back on your feet, you are free to go. You have my word."

"I believe you."

He gave her a cup of the deer's blood and said, "Here."

She grabbed the cup and said, "This is getting old. Eventually, I'm going to need real fresh blood." She drank the deer's blood, then put the cup down on the table and said, "I'm going to sleep. I'll see you in the morning." Princess Ariel rolled over and went to sleep. Kaiden lay on the floor and went to sleep as well.

## The fourth day

Back at the kingdom of Cumberland, King Philip was speaking with his generals in the throne hall, sitting in his throne chair. He said to them as they stood in front of their king, "Any word of my daughter?"

"No, my king. We looked for her everywhere but have not yet found her, and there are no signs that she's even alive."

King Philip was frustrated and said, "Are you trying to tell me that my daughter, my princess, could be dead?"

"No, my king," the general's voice trembled as he answered.

"Then get your ass back out there and find my daughter! Before I have your head up a horse's ass!"

"Yes, sir, right away, my king."

Then King Philip yelled out to his assistant.

"Yes, my king?"

"Get Lord Gerald here, immediately!"

"As you wish, my king." The assistant left the throne hall, and then Queen Helen entered the throne hall and said, "I heard you yelling as I was going by. Is everything all right with our daughter?"

He answered and said, "Yes, dear, please do not worry. Everything is fine. She is a trained warrior."

"I hope so," she left the throne hall.

Hours later, Lord Gerald arrived at King Philip's castle in the throne hall. Lord Gerald said to the king, "You have summoned me?"

"Yes, I did. Can you tell me what went wrong?"

Lord Gerald looked at the king and said, "My nephew interfered."

"Your nephew interfered? Did I not ask you if he would be a concern? Did I?"

"Yes, you did," Lord Gerald looked away from the king.

You could hear the frustration in the king's voice as he said, "And now my daughter is missing."

Lord Gerald looked back at the king and said, "My apologies."

"Keep your apology. The price you pay monthly just went up until my daughter returns home. And if I find out she is dead, it will be doubled. Do you understand?"

"Yes."

"You are dismissed!"

## The fifth day

Princess Ariel sat on the bed, and Prince Kaiden sat next to her, checking her wounds. He said, "They're getting better."

She said to him, "Good, I'll be on my way soon. I'm pretty sure my father and mother are worried sick about me."

He said, "You shall return home very soon."

Then she looked at him and said, "But I still don't understand. How can someone like you be so powerful, yet be so kind?"

He looked at her and answered, "I am a man of peace. We lived in this world together, why fight over it?"

"I see why Abel chose you, but you do know, once we walk out that door, we are enemies. My father wishes to have your land."

"We don't have to be enemies, Ariel. But I understand. You wish to respect your father's wishes."

"You dressed my wounds. You fed me horse shit and deer blood." Kaiden smiled and chuckled, and she continued to say, "You even clothed me and nourished me back to health, and I thank you for repaying you back with my sword. What kind of vampire woman does that make me?"

"You are who you choose to be."

She looked at him with stars in her eyes; he looked back at her, and they kissed. He grabbed her by the waist; she placed her head on the side of his face. And they kissed deeper, and they lay down on the bed. They undress each other and make love. That night, they fell deeply in love with each other, and they lay in bed to…

## The next morning

They woke up in bed together, facing each other, resting their arms on each other. She said with a "rise and shine" smile, "Good morning, my handsome man."

He replied, "Good morning, my lady."

She asked him, "What are we eating today?"

"Hungry already?" he asked.

"I did just wake up."

He reached over to play with her ear and said, "Umm. I was thinking of hunting babirusa."

She licked her lips and said, "Sounds delicious. I've never had babirusa's blood before."

He got out of bed and put his clothes on. She sat up and said to him, "You know my wounds would have healed a lot faster if I had human blood."

As he was getting dressed, he looked at her and said, "I know, my love. I know. And I'm sorry."

"It's okay, baby. I understand," she said to him. "Where did you find this cabin?"

He sat down in the chair and said, "When we played as kids, Shymair, Jessica, and I, we used to pretend we were lost travelers, and we stumbled across this very cabin for shelter."

She looked at him and said, "I remember when you said I remind you of someone. Who?"

"Yes, Jessica." He looked away and then said, "She was very ill, I could not save her, she passed away. She was my best friend." He looked back at her and said, "Like a sister to me."

She got out of bed, put her clothes on, and said, "It's not your fault, you did what you could, and Jessica lives on through you." After she was done putting her clothes on, she sat on the edge of the bed and said, "She's in your heart. You're a werewolf and spiritually connected with Yeshua's nature. You know better than to think someone is truly gone."

He got up and said, "I haven't been meditating to feel her spirit or anyone else's because of the pain, but that feels good to know."

She got up, walked toward him, hugged him, and said, "Hey, we have each other now."

He gently placed both of his hands on the side of her face, kissed her, and said, "Yes, we do."

She wrapped her arms around him and said, "But we must play it safe. Our fathers are enemies. We cannot pretend we're living in this fairy tale story like everything is okay."

He said to her, "When I leave this cabin, you will be in my heart, mind, and soul."

She looked up at him and said, "Even when you are sworn to be married to the one your father has chosen for you?"

He looked down at her and said, "How can I be with someone when my heart lies with another?"

She went to sit in the chair and said, looking at him, "I have faith in us."

He smiled and said, "As do I."

Then hours later, Kaiden went for his hunt and brought back dinner. He cut it open and cooked it. When they were done eating, they lay in bed, holding each other. She said, "I wish this could last forever," and he replied, "Me too, love." And they slept until…

*The next morning*

When morning came, they decided it would be safe for them to leave at night. Princess Ariel was a vampire and could not be in the sun, and later that night, the moon was big and bright. Princess Ariel and Prince Kaiden were getting ready to leave the cabin. They walked outside; he walked toward his horse, and she followed behind him. He turned around and said to her, "Here. Take my horse." She looked at the horse, gently rubbed the horse, and said, "It's a very beautiful horse." She looked back at him and said, "Are you sure, my love?"

He answered, "Yes, my love. I am."

"How are you going to return back home?" she asked.

"I'll walk back," he answered.

She slowly reached over to kiss him on the cheek and whispered in his ear, saying, "You are your kind." He grabbed her by the waist, kissed her on the lips, and then looked at her, saying, "I will miss you," and she replied, "I miss you."

He picked her up and put her on the horse, saying, "We shall meet back here one week from today."

He walked back from the horse and said, "I can't wait."

She rode off, he watched her as she rode, and he smiled and said to himself, *Now I understand what my father told me the day we were on the mountain.*

Then Kaiden jogged back to Galloway.

Princess Ariel returned to her homeland of Cumberland; the vampires bowed as she was riding through the community. She arrived at the castle, and one of the guards said to her, "Princess Ariel! Your father has been expecting you. Come with me. I will announce your arrival."

King Philip was in the throne hall, sitting in his royal chair, drinking a cup of blood. The guard entered the throne room and said to the king, "Princess Ariel has arrived."

The king was happily surprised to see his daughter. When she came into the throne room, the king put the cup down, stood up, and said, "Good son of the dragon, where have you been? Your mother and I have been worried about you."

She said, "I am fine, Father. I was deeply wounded, so I took refuge. When I recovered, I returned home immediately."

King Philip walked toward his daughter, hugged her, looked at her with joy, and said, "I'm glad you're all right. I love you so much."

"I love you too, Father."

"Now. Please, go see your mother at once."

"Yes."

Later that same night, Prince Kaiden finally made it to his homeland of Galloway. Werewolf guards guarding the gate saw someone coming and began to growl, showing their sharp teeth, looking scared and ready to attack. "It is I, Prince Kaiden!"

The werewolf guards stopped growling and allowed Kaiden to pass; they bowed their heads. He arrived at the castle, entered inside, and saw the help doing late-night dusting, Kaiden said to her, "Excuse me."

She turned around and said, "Oh, Prince Kaiden. Your mother and father have been worried about you."

"Where are they?" he asked.

"Follow me."

Kaiden followed her, King Ka'Ron and Queen Lawanda were in the kitchen, sitting at the table having a late-night snack. The help walked in first and said, "My king and queen, the prince is here."

Then Kaiden walked into the kitchen, and the king said, "Where have you been, my boy?"

He answered, "After the battle was won, I decided to search the land to see if there were any more of our enemies still lurking."

The queen said, "You have done well, my son."

"Thank you, Mother and Father."

The king got up, placed his hand on Kaiden's shoulder, and said, "I'm glad you made it home, my son." The queen got up and hugged Kaiden; he hugged her back, kissed him on the cheek, and she said, "I missed you, son," and he said, "I missed you, Mother." The queen sat back down at the table, and the king looked at him and said, "You may go to your room and get yourself cleaned up."

"Thank you, Father." Kaiden left the kitchen, the king said to the queen, "Honey, I can't help but feel that your son is lying to me about his whereabouts. His voice sounds rattled."

The queen asked, "What reason does he need to lie?"

He looked at her and said, "I don't know, that's what troubles my thoughts."

Back at Cumberland, Ariel went to see her mother. The queen was sitting at her desk, brushing her hair in the mirror. Then the queen heard a knock at the door, and she said, "You may come in."

Ariel opened the door and said, "Mother." The queen turned around and saw her daughter. The queen felt a warm sense of happiness when her eyes met her daughter's. The queen quickly got up and rushed toward her with a joyful relief, and they embraced each other with a hug. The queen said, "I missed you, my baby." Princess Ariel said, "And I missed you, Mother."

The queen looked at her and asked, "Did you tell your father where you have been?"

Ariel answered, "Yes."

"Good, good. I'm so glad you're home and safe." The queen grabbed her by the face and then said, "You look exhausted."

Ariel said, "I am, Mother."

"Well then, you go to your room and get some rest. We can talk in the morning."

"Will do, Mother." Ariel left her mother's bedroom and headed toward her room. When she got there, she made herself comfortable and went to sleep.

Back at Galloway, Kaiden entered his room, cleaned himself up, lay in bed, and went to sleep.

# Chapter 6

# Forbidden Love

*A few days had passed*

In the middle of the night, Prince Kaiden was in his room, lying in bed, looking at the bright moon, thinking of Princess Ariel. Kaiden missed her; he longed for her touch. *I must see her*, he thought to himself. Then someone knocked on his door. "Who's knocking?" Kaiden asked.

"It's your sister, Adrianna."

"You may enter."

He got up and sat on the bed. She opened the door and walked into his room.

Kaiden asked, "What brings you to me, big sister?"

And she said, "I came to make sure you were all right. You were just in a battle a week ago, then absent for a few days."

Kaiden looked at her and said, "Yes, my sister. I'm all right. I appreciate your concern."

Adrianna folded her hands together by her waist and said, "I was worried for you. I do not like violence, even though we are creatures of violence."

"Indeed, we are. But I assure you, I'm all right. May I ask a favor of you?"

"Of course, brother."

"I'm going out tonight. If anyone asks, tell them I couldn't sleep, so I went for a walk."

She asked, "Where might you go for the night?"

Kaiden looked at her with a smile and said, "Somewhere peaceful."

She said, "Be safe, little brother."

She left his room and closed the door behind her. Kaiden got out of bed and changed his clothes. He jumped from his window and landed quietly on the ground. He went to the stable, grabbed a horse, and rode off into the night.

But moments before Kaiden left, Lord Gerald said to his consulting, "I have an errand for you."

"Where am I being sent to, my lord?" the consulting asked.

Lord Gerald handed him a chest box of silver coins and gold and said, "Payment for King Philip."

The consulting grabbed the chest box and said, "Yes, my lord. I will be leaving you now." Then the consulting told one of the guards to fetch the horse wagon and said to the guard, "We are traveling to Cumberland to see King Philip." The consulting and guard rode off into the night.

Princess Ariel was in her bedroom, sitting at her dresser, reading a book and drinking blood from a wineglass. Then she heard, "Hey, my dove."

She was startled and turned around, noticing it was Kaiden at her window. She said, "How did you get here? I didn't even hear you come in."

He got down from the window and said, "Well then, it's a good thing we're not enemies. Without a thought, I would cut your throat. As you put it."

She got up with a smile, and they rushed toward each other. They hugged and kissed, and then they sat on the bed, and she said, "How did you get past the guards?"

"I move fast and quite unnoticed, and I rushed all for you."

"How charming."

"You were on my mind, like a heavy brick. I needed to see you."

She looked at him and said, "You're always on my mind."

They gazed at each other and kissed. He gripped her and kissed her neck, saying, "I want you." And she said, "I need you."

Then suddenly, a knock at the door. They startled and immediately stopped. "Who is it?" she asked.

"It's your mother. I heard a voice coming from your room. Are you all right? I'm about to come in."

Ariel and Kaiden quickly got up. Ariel said, "Just a minute! I'm not decent." She looked at Kaiden and whispered quietly, "Time to go."

She rushed him toward the window, and he said, "Let us meet tomorrow."

"Yes, of course. Now go," she said in a quiet, hasty voice.

They went by the window, and her mother said, "Honey, are you almost done? I'm about to come in."

Kaiden was almost out the window, and Princess Ariel said, "Just one second!" Kaiden climbed out the window and jumped. When he landed, he looked up at her and said, "At the cabin," and she said, "Yes, my love. I'll be there."

He smiled at her, and then he jumped to another roof. Within a second, her mother opened the door.

Princess Ariel quickly turned around from the window, and her mother said, "I couldn't wait any longer. Are you all right?"

"Yes, Mother."

"Why are you standing by the window?" her mother asked.

She quickly thought of words to speak and said, "Oh, I was getting some fresh air."

"Well, come away from there."

"Yes, Mother."

Before Princess Ariel walked away from the window, she looked to see if Kaiden was still there on the roof he had jumped to. But he was already gone in the wind. Princess Ariel's nerves calmed down, and she was at ease. She said, "I'm coming, Mother."

She walked by the bed and stood by the bed footboard, and her mother said, "I heard voices in here. Who were you speaking with?"

"No one, myself."

The mother laughed a little and said, "Yourself, darling, are you ill?"

"No, Mother. Just lost in deep thoughts."

Queen Helen folded both her hands by her side and said, "All right then, I'll leave you to it. Good night."

"Good night, Mother."

Queen Helen walked out of the room and closed the door behind her. Princess Ariel took a deep breath, fell into her bed with her arms open, and ended her night.

Moments before Kaiden sneaked into Ariel's room, the consulting arrived at King Philip's castle with his payment. The guards opened the gate and let him enter the castle. The guard approached the consulting and grabbed the box from him. The guard said, "Follow me, I'll escort you to the king."

King Philip was in the throne hall when the consulting and the guard arrived. The king said, "Right on time. You can place it right there. And oh, consulting, tell Lord Gerald, I'll attack again in two days' time."

The consulting looked at him and said, "I'll tell Lord Gerald immediately."

Then the king said, "And, consulting?"

"Yes?"

"If something goes wrong again, my price goes up."

"As you wish, King Philip."

King Philip raised his right finger and said, "Before you go, I ask you, what is your real name?"

The consulting chuckled and said, "We have no name, just given many names. We are Legion, for we are many and the purpose of our service, for we set our goals on the heart and mind of men, while Yeshua wastes his time trying to save their souls. That is my name."

The king looked at him and said, "I suppose. You may leave me now."

The consulting left King Philip's castle and headed back toward his horse wagon. He told the rider, "We will be leaving now."

As the consulting was leaving and passing through the gates, he noticed Prince Kaiden fleeing from King Philip's castle. He thought to himself, *What is he doing here?* in a concerned voice. He traveled back to Galloway. When he returned, he spoke with Lord Gerald, saying, "My lord, I have done what you asked."

"Excellent," Lord Gerald said.

"King Philip informed me to tell you he will attack again within two days' time. And if anything goes wrong, he will double the price."

"That hungry greedy bastard!" He slammed his hand against the wall. He then said, "Vampires don't just suck your blood, they suck every piece of silver and gold you have." He sat down in a chair and rubbed his head, feeling great distress. He continued, "I patiently wait for the time to come when I drive a stake through his heart."

"Also, my lord, returning from my travels, I saw Prince Kaiden sneaking out from King Philip's castle."

"How suspicious," Lord Gerald said, looking confused. He asked, "Did he see you?"

"No, I was inconspicuous."

"Good. Now why would that little shit be doing there? I wonder."

"I don't know, my lord."

"We shall watch him closely. Have one of ours follow him."

"Excellent idea, my lord. I will attempt to do it immediately."

"You may leave me for the night."

"Yes, my lord."

The consulting left the room, and Lord Gerald ended his night. Finally, Prince Kaiden returned home and climbed up to his window, returning to his room.

### The next day

At night, on a beautiful night the moon was big, bright, and shining, King Philip was in the war room with his generals, discussing the plan for the next attack on King Ka'Ron. Each of them was given a cup of blood but could not drink until they discussed the war plan. Then the king noticed Princess Ariel was absent from the war room. King Philip yelled out for the help, "*Assistant! Assistant!*"

The help entered the war room, standing by the door with her hands folded across her waist and her head down, and the help said in a nervous voice, "Yes, my king? You have summoned me?"

King Philip looked at her and said, "Send for my daughter, she is needed in the war room. *Now!*"

"Yes, my king," the help quickly left the war room, heading toward Princess Ariel's room. She knocked on her door and said, "Princess Ariel, Princess Ariel, your father wishes to see you." The help knocked again and said, "Forgive me for coming in, but your father would like to see you." The help slowly opened the door, saying in a soft voice, "Princess Ariel." When she peeked into her room, she saw that Princess Ariel was not there; she was gone. The help closed the door and quickly headed back toward King Philip in the war room. As the help entered the war room, she approached the king and whispered in his ear, "Princess Ariel is not in her room."

The king whispered back in the help's ear, saying, "Find her, she's here somewhere."

"Yes, my king."

As the help was leaving the war room, one of the generals asked, "Is everything all right, my king?"

The king stood up from the war table and said with his arms open, "Yes, everything is fine. Please, drink. It's fresh blood."

A different general said, "We cannot do business without Princess Ariel."

The king was a little annoyed by what his general had just said to him, and he responded, "I am aware, have patience! My daughter will be here." Then the king sat back down.

All the assistants in the castle gathered to look for Princess Ariel; they searched throughout the whole castle and outside. The same help came back to the war room and approached the king, whispering in his ear, "She's not here, my king. We looked everywhere. She's gone."

King Philip looked at the help and yelled, "*She's gone?*"

The help was scared and quickly backed up from the king. She said to the king, "Yes, perhaps she left."

"Where the hell is she?" the king asked.

Some of the generals shook their heads as if they were disappointed.

Moments before the king needed his daughter, Princess Ariel crept out of her room to meet her lover, Prince Kaiden, at the cabin as they had planned. She sat on the bed, patiently waiting for Kaiden to arrive. Minutes later, she heard a horse galloping; she smiled and got up, heading out the door. She saw Kaiden riding his horse toward her. Kaiden stopped his horse, dismounted, and quickly rushed to her.

She said to him as he approached her, "Finally, you are here," with excitement.

He responded, "My love." They embraced each other with a hug and a kiss. She looked at him as they hugged and said, "Hello, my prince," and he looked at her and replied, "Hello, my princess." Then Kaiden said to her, "Let's go inside and enjoy ourselves," and she agreed, saying, "Yes, love." Kaiden picked her up and carried her inside the cabin. He laid her down on the bed, and they made love. However, Kaiden was unaware that someone had followed him from a distance, creeping quietly like a mouse—a watcher from Lord Gerald. Kaiden was so happy to be on his way to see his love that he didn't even notice he was being followed. The unknown watcher stayed out there, continuing to watch them from far away. Afterward, Princess Ariel and Prince Kaiden cuddled and fell asleep, holding each other until…

## The next day

Back in the land of Cumberland, King Philip was in the throne hall, sitting in his throne chair. The king was very furious because he still had not yet found his daughter. He had all the grounds and soldiers searching and looking for her. Queen Helen was in her room, worried about her daughter being absent. King Philip looked at his grounds as they stood in front of him and said, "The next one who comes back and tells me they still haven't found my daughter, I am going to burn them in the sun!"

*Meanwhile*

"Good afternoon, my love," Kaiden said to Ariel, as she slowly woke up, still half-asleep, and she said to him, "Mmm, good afternoon."

Then suddenly, she fully woke up, jumped up, and said, "Oh, shit! I fucking overslept." She quickly got out of bed and jumped over Kaiden as he was still laying down.

He said, "Baby, slow down," as she was rushing to put on her clothes.

She said, "How am I going to explain this one? My father is going to kill me."

Kaiden sat up off the bed and said, "Baby, everything will be okay."

When she was done getting dressed, she said, "My mother is probably worried sick, she is a worried vampire woman."

Kaiden got out of bed, put his clothes on, and walked toward her. He placed both of his hands on her shoulder, looked at her, and said, "Hey, don't stress yourself out, we can figure something out."

She looked back at him and said, "I can't even leave because the sun is up."

Kaiden kissed her on the cheek and said, "Wait here, stay out of the sun, I shall return."

As he was leaving the cabin, he was almost out the door when she asked him, "Where are you going?"

Kaiden turned around, looked at her, and replied, "To help you figure this out."

He walked out the door and headed toward his horse. He got on the horse and took off. A good hour later, Kaiden finally returned with a horse buggy with the windows covered from the sun. He climbed down from the horse buggy, walked inside the cabin, and found Ariel sitting in a chair, staying out of the range of the sun. Even though the windows were covered, and the sunlight was able to hit the floor, she kept her distance.

Kaiden said to her, "You can ride in this, it will keep you safe from the sun."

71

She smiled at him and said, "You are a clever man, I knew I loved you for a reason."

Then she noticed Kaiden looked a little disturbed, so she asked him, "What's wrong?"

He replied, "Nothing. It's just my wolf senses keep telling me someone is watching us, but I have been ignoring it because I've been worried about getting you home. But I'm pretty sure it's nothing."

"I hope so," she said.

Then he said, "When you get in the horse buggy, stay on the path. It's a smart horse, it will take you home."

"That's the second horse you gave me."

"Who's counting? But are you ready to go?"

She said, "Yes."

He grabbed the blanket off the bed to cover her, protecting her from the sun. Before he covered her, she said, "If my father asks, I have to come up with a story of where I've been."

He tossed the blanket around her and said, "You will come up with something."

Ariel grabbed his hand, and in distress, she said, "That's the thing, Kaiden. How long do I have to keep coming up with fake stories, lying to my father and mother? How long do we have to keep secretly seeing each other? How long is this fairytale going to last with us? And at the end of the day, our fathers are sworn enemies. How long do we have to pretend that we are enemies? And when this war is over between our fathers, you are promised to marry the king's richest daughter." Ariel became even more distressed, and her eyes changed. She said, "And do you really think I'm supposed to be okay at night knowing you're laid up with another woman?"

Kaiden gently grabbed her by the chin and said, "Baby, look into my eyes." When she did, her eyes turned back to normal, and she calmed down. He said, "I may be promised to another, but my heart, mind, and soul are promised to you. I promise we will figure something out."

She looked down and said, "I hope you're right." Then she looked up at him and said, "Because we are cursed and blessed. The devil blesses us vampires with eternal life. And then Yahweh cursed us monsters. Made us weak to silver, wood, sunlight. Cut us deep enough by werewolf's claws, and it takes weeks to heal properly. All thanks to Dracula the Impaler for making a deal with a demon. And the elder vampires made it the law that it's an abomination for vampires and werewolves to cross species. You will be put to death."

Kaiden felt joy in him and gently placed both of his hands on the sides of her face. He said, "I am aware of the risk, and I am willing to accept the punishment that comes with it. I have Yeshua in me."

She looked at him with deep love and said, "Then we shall see this until the end, my love."

"Now let us leave." Then Kaiden fully covered her up with the blanket from head to toe.

He kept her covered and walked her out the door, heading toward the horse buggy. He opened the door for her, she got inside, and he closed the door. Then he smacked the horse on the hindquarters, telling the horse to go, and the horse took off. When the horse buggy was out of Kaiden's sight, he began to walk back home to the land of Galloway.

Moments later, Princess Ariel made it back to her homeland, Cumberland. The horse buggy was stopped at the gate by familiar guards who guarded the gate during sunlight hours. "*Who goes there?*" the familiar guard yelled.

"It is I, Princess Ariel!"

Then the familiar guard said, "Open the gate, the princess is passing through!" They opened the gate for her, and the familiar guard yelled out to the other familiars, "The princess is passing through, pass the word along to announce her arrival to the king!"

King Philip was in his room with his wife, Queen Hellen, and one of the familiars went to inform King Philip of his daughter's arrival. The familiar guard knocked on the king's door, and the king said, "Who dares to disturb the queen and me at sunlight hours?"

"My king, it is your daughter. She has arrived."

King Philip said, "You may enter." The familiar opened the door and walked inside, saying, "My king and queen, Princess Ariel is here."

The king said, "Tell my daughter to meet me in the throne hall at once."

"Yes, my king," the familiar left the king's room immediately, and Queen Hellen said, "I hope she's all right."

Then the horse buggy stopped in front of the castle. She grabbed the blanket and covered herself from the sun. The familiar guard opened the horse buggy door for her, and she got out, tossing the blanket away. Then one of the familiar guards approached her and said, "Your father wishes to see you in the throne hall; please follow me."

As Ariel followed the familiar, she was nervous to see her father. Her mind was racing quickly to think of words to say and not to say. Her father was furious with her as he waited in the throne hall, sitting in his throne chair.

The familiar guard walked in and said, "Your majesty, Princess Ariel has arrived."

She walked into the throne room, looking shameful. The king waved the familiar guard away with his hand and said, "Leave us." The familiar guard turned around and left, shutting the big door behind him. King Philip looked at her with fiery red eyes and said, "You were sent for, we needed you in the war room. Your absence has shown me that you are incapable of leading my army. You went missing on the battlefield, and your mother is worried about your disappearance. I don't have the patience anymore to keep her at ease. You have exhausted my men's time looking for you."

Princess Ariel said in an emotional voice, "Father, please forgive me. I can exp—"

King Philip cut her off before she had the chance to explain and said, "Spare me your words."

She said, "But, Father, please."

The king's eyes turned bloody dark red and shouted, "*I said spare me your words!*"

She bowed her head toward the ground, and the king said, "You made me look like a fool in front of my generals when you are the one in charge."

She soaked in tears and did not lift her head as she said in an emotional voice, "I never meant to dishonor you, Father."

And the king said, "As of this moment, I wish not to know where you were or what you were doing. Go to your room. Now leave me."

Princess Ariel turned around and walked toward the big door.

Before she walked out, her father said, "Make sure you are in your room when I send for you."

She didn't look up and said, "Yes, Father." She left the throne hall and went to her room.

Back in the land of Galloway, the one who had been watching Ariel and Kaiden at the cabin made it back before Kaiden did. Lord Gerald was in his room, sitting at his desk, writing in his books.

His consulting knocked on Lord Gerald's door and said, "Come in."

The consulting opened the door and walked in. He said, "My lord."

"Yes?"

The consulting approached closely and said, "The one you seek to watch has arrived."

"Speak of it."

The watcher said, "Prince Kaiden is secretly seeing Princess Ariel."

Lord Gerald was shocked by what he had just heard and said, "Are your words true?"

"Yes, my lord, I speak the truth."

"How the hell did they start seeing each other?"

"I don't know, my lord."

"Where do they go for each other?"

"They see each other at an abandoned cabin far in the woods, about thirty-five miles from here."

"This is excellent news. You have done well. Make sure you speak of this to no one but me. Do you understand?"

"Yes, my lord, I shall do so."

Lord Gerald handed the one who had been watching thirty pieces of silver and said, "You may leave me now."

A few minutes later, Prince Kaiden finally made it back to his homeland, Galloway. When he entered the castle, one of the helpers approached him and said, "Oh, Prince Kaiden. I was just about to come look for you."

Kaiden looked at the helper and asked, "And why is that?"

And the helper said, "Your father sent me for you, they're waiting for you in the throne room."

"Thank you, I shall go."

Kaiden walked toward the throne room. When he walked inside, King Ka'Ron and his generals, Lord Gerald, and his consulting were all waiting for Prince Kaiden. The king said, "Son, join us, sit."

Kaiden sat down and said, "What is this gathering, Father?"

King Ka'Ron looked at Lord Gerald and said, "Brother, please explain to your nephew."

Lord Gerald looked at Kaiden and said, "We located King Philip's army camp."

"Where?" Kaiden asked.

Lord Gerald answered, "Just about fifty-two miles from here, heading west."

Then Kaiden asked, "How was the camp discovered?"

One of the generals said, "By one of our scouts."

And then King Ka'Ron said, "We attack tomorrow at dawn, burn their tents with flying fire arrows. When they run out, the sun will blaze them into fire as we swing our claws at their necks."

"Sounds like a wonderful plan," Kaiden said.

And the general said, "And of course, you will lead us into the battle."

Kaiden looked at the general and said, "Another victory we should have had."

And the king said, "Then it is settled. Everyone is dismissed."

Kaiden got up and walked out. His mind was on Ariel, hoping she would not be there at tomorrow's attack. He went to his room and got his thoughts together.

After the gathering in the throne hall, Lord Gerald and his consulting were having a secret conversation outside the castle. "I get word from our eyes and ears. Prince Kaiden is secretly seeing Princess Ariel."

The consulting said, "King Philip's vampire daughter is secretly seeing a werewolf prince. That's a death sentence."

"Kaiden is supposed to marry King Richard's daughter, Evelyn. He will wage war upon my brother for his son denying his daughter's hand in marriage."

"Indeed, he will."

"I need a meeting tonight with King Philip. Send word to his people, tell them it's urgent. I must speak with him at once."

"Yes, my lord."

*Later that night*

When Lord Gerald received his invitation, he traveled to Cumberland to speak with King Philip. The guards let him through the gate, and he was escorted to the king. He arrived in the throne hall, and the guard said, "Lord Gerald, your majesty."

King Philip said, "You request an audience with me?"

Lord Gerald said, "Yes. It's my words to share with you privately."

King Philip clapped his hands and said, "Everyone leave. Now!"

When everyone left the throne hall, he said, "Speak."

Lord Gerald said, "My brother discovered your military camp from one of his scouts. There are planned attacks tomorrow at noon. The plan is to burn the tents, draw your men out, and cut their throats as they scald from the sun."

Then the king said, "Excellent. Sounds like everything's going according to plan."

"Of course, the scout works for me."

And the king said, "We shall use this opportunity against them for a final blow, bringing this to an end, killing your brother."

Then Lord Gerald said, "There's something."

The king asked, "And what?"

"I have been suspicious of my nephew, so I put someone on him to watch him."

"And?"

"They have come to inform me that my nephew has been secretly seeing your daughter romantically."

King Philip said in disbelief, "You lie."

"I speak the truth. Your daughter is seeing Kaiden. Secretly."

King Philip stood up from his throne chair and walked toward Lord Gerald, saying, "Speak everything. Now."

"They have been secretly seeing each other in an abandoned cabin late at night."

King Philip turned his back and faced Lord Gerald, and the king looked over his shoulder and said, "How did this happen?"

Before Lord Gerald answered, King Philip sat back down. "I only know they sometimes stay in the cabin. Like this morning, my nephew left her there, and he returned with a—"

"Horse buggy."

"Yes. That is correct."

As King Philip sat in his chair and tried to think of all the possibilities of how his daughter started seeing Prince Kaiden, Lord Gerald said, "I'm only telling you this because I wish for your daughter to stay away from my nephew. This can only endanger what I have planned. This is what I wish to tell you in private, King Philip. Because of the law of crossbreed, the punishment is death."

The king turned his head quickly with fiery eyes, looked at him, and said, "I'm aware of the punishment! Who else knows of this?"

"Just me and my intel, and now you."

"Keep it that way, or I'll have your head. Now, anything else you need to tell me?"

"No."

"Then my generals will send you word of how we will kill your brother tomorrow. You may go now."

Lord Gerald left from King Philip's castle and traveled back to Galloway. The king held his head with his hand, with distress upon him of how his daughter started seeing Prince Kaiden. He said to himself, "The battlefield," and then the king said, "She betrayed me."

King Philip got up from his chair and headed toward Princess Ariel's room. When he arrived, he told the two guards who were guarding her door to leave. When the guards left, the king opened her door. Ariel was sitting on her bed, and when she saw her father enter her room unannounced, she stood up. The look he was giving her, she could tell something was wrong, and she said, "Father?"

"Is it true?"

Princess Ariel looked at her father with a confused face and said, "Is what true you ask of me?"

The king pointed his finger at her and said, "You dare to look at me and act like you know not what I say."

"Father, please speak plainly."

"You have been romantically involved with a lycanthrope."

Ariel acted like she was shocked and said, "Foolish words for you to speak of."

The king approached her and got closer, and he said, "I want to believe you, I really do, but your absence clouds my trust for you."

Ariel turned her back toward her father, and she faced the window said, "Father, I'm sorry for my absence that has caused your trust in me. I have good reasons for disappearing. But this accusation that you are accusing me of is not true." King Philip approached her closer from behind her, and she continued to say, "Of me being romantically involved with Prince Kaiden. That is silly and ridiculous."

He laid his hand on her shoulder and said, "My daughter?"

As his hand was on her shoulder, she reached for his hand and placed her hand on top of his hand, and she said, "Yes, father?"

And he said, "I never told you his name."

The king bit her on the neck, tasting her blood on his tongue. He saw everything she had been doing through echo vision. The king was able to see she had been secretly seeing Kaiden and everything else she had been doing. When the echo vision was over, she turned around in a panic and saw her father's eyes turn bloody red, and he said to her in a raging yelling voice, "*You have lied to me! To be with a fucking dog!*"

The king grabbed her by the neck, picked her up, and threw her. She hit the wall, which cracked, and she fell to the floor. She said in a crying voice, "Father, please. Don't be angry with me."

And the king said in a raging yelling voice, "*You have sacrificed everything you worked for! To be with a fucking filthy animal!*"

Ariel got up off the floor with her eyes watery and said, "Father. *Please!* I beg of you."

And the king said, "It's just not about you throwing everything away, you worked for. You can be executed for this crime." The king looked away from her and said, "My own flesh and blood will have to face judgment." The king looked back at her and said, "You have put your own life in danger, and for what? To be with a *dog*! No, the generals and accountants cannot hear of this."

Ariel looked at her father in shock, and then the king continued to say, "For tomorrow, that boy and his father will be dead."

"How is that?" she asked as she was curious.

"They will arrive at my military camp, thinking it's empty, and we shall have the element of surprise, easily killing them, a trap."

And then Ariel said, "Father, please. I love him."

With rage in the king's eyes, he said, "The forbidden love you have for that wet dog! Is a betrayal to me and your duty as princess to this kingdom."

"I didn't betray you, Father. It just happened, it could be a faith from Yeshua."

The king grabbed her by the neck again and picked her up in the air; her feet dangled, and the king said, "You would dare not put the God, Yeshua, in this. For you have crossed species, that *sin* is an *abomination*!"

The king was choking her, and she tried to gasp for air, and the king said, "That boy and his father will be dead by tomorrow, and you will forget about this boy, and you will speak none of this nonsense, *no more*!"

The king threw her on the bed; she was coughing for air. King Philip left her room and locked her door from the outside and had the guards guarding the door, and the king said to the guards, "Princess Ariel is not leaving this room until I say otherwise."

As Princess Ariel could hear her father yelling outside her door to the guards, soaking her eyes in tears, she said to herself, *I'm sorry, Father, but I cannot allow this. I love Prince Kaiden to death. For I will sacrifice my life for his, and I know he will do the same for me. I must warn him.*

Ariel grabbed her black chest body armor and strapped it on, then she grabbed her black arm and leg armor and strapped it on. She grabbed her sword and shuriken, which was used to throw dagger stars. She wrapped her hair in a ponytail and yelled, *"Guards! Guards!"*

The two guards look at each other. "Should we go?"

"Maybe."

"I go."

The guard came into the room and said, "Is everything all right?"

She hit him over the head, knocking him unconscious. Then the other guard came into the room and saw the guard knocked out on the floor and said, "What the fuck!"

She threw a shuriken at his head; he fell to his knees and burned. She peeked her head out the door to see if anyone is coming; it's a clear view of her escape, and she quietly sneaked out of the castle, passing the guards. She creeped up behind a guard and choked him until he passed out; she stole one of the horses, hopped on, and took off, riding as fast as she could through the night. She arrived in the land of Galloway, four werewolf soldiers guarding the pathway at the entrance like guard dogs.

One of the guards saw someone coming riding a horse fast and said, "Announce yourself, stranger!"

Ariel didn't respond; she continued to ride fast, and the guard said again, "Announce yourself!"

Ariel still didn't respond; she continued to ride fast. The guard who asked transformed with the other three werewolves; two of them charged at her. She rode faster and gripped on the horse straps and stood on the saddle. The two werewolves jumped up off the ground and charged toward her in the air. Ariel's eyes turned dark red, and she unsheathed two of her wrist blades and jumped off the horse in the air and cut both of their throats and landed on the ground, her blade dripping with their blood.

The other two werewolf soldiers charged at her; she quickly pulled two of her shuriken from the holster and threw them at the third one, piercing his head. He hit the ground, and then she moved like a shadow, appearing behind the fourth one, cutting the were-wolf's throat. The horse ran past her; she ran and hopped on the horse.

Then minutes later, she arrived at the castle. She sneaked her way in by scaling the walls; she reached Kaiden's window and climbed in. Kaiden wasn't in his room, so she hid and waited for him.

Back at Cumberland, a guard passed Ariel's room and saw ashes of the dead vampire and a guard unconscious. He woke the guard up and said, "What happened here?"

The guard got up slowly and said, "Princess Ariel has escaped."

"Ohhh, shit." He ran to King Philip and said, "My king!"

The king said, "What?"

"Princess Ariel has escaped!"

The king was now angry and said, "I should have expected this."

"What are your orders, sir?"

The king closed his eyes, drank his glass of blood wine, and said calmly as he was slow to anger, "Nothing."

## Moments later

Kaiden walked into his room, and she popped out from behind him like a shadow ghost. He quickly turned around, grabbed her by the neck, his claws piercing her throat, and she swiftly said, "My love, it's me!"

He removed his claw from her throat and said, "I could have killed you, I got word of an intruder, four soldiers are dead."

"That was me."

Kaiden looked confused and said, "I don't understand."

And she said to him, "I came here to warn you, please, love. You must listen to me."

He looked at her with passion and said, "Speak, my love."

"My father knows of us, I don't know how he found out." Kaiden looked at her in shock, and then she continued to say, "My father was angry with me, he almost killed me."

"Are you hurt?" Kaiden asked.

She said, "I'm fine, but listen. He knows your father is planning to attack his military camp tomorrow. My father is planning an ambush. Don't go!"

And then Kaiden said, "I must bring this news to my father. Come with me at once."

She asked, "Is going to your father a good idea?"

"He will ask me, where did I get my source, once we tell him this, he will come to reason."

And she said, "I trust you."

"And besides, your father knows of us. I believe it's time for my father to know of us as well, if it causes my life to be with you, then let the price of my life be with you."

"Okay, my love." They kissed.

And he said, "My father is in the throne room."

They left his room, heading toward the throne room. When they arrived at the throne room, they were standing by the door before they entered inside; he looked at her and asked, "Are you ready?"

She looked back at him and said, "Yes."

They held each other's hand and entered the throne room. King Ka'Ron was going over paperwork with his brother, Lord Gerald. "Father, I must speak with you at once."

King Ka'Ron stood up from the table and said, "What is this? What the hell is she doing here?"

Lord Gerald had an "oh shit" look on his face.

They approached, and Kaiden said, "Father, please hear my words."

The king asked, "Boy! Do you know who this woman is?"

Then King Ka'Ron looked and noticed the two of them were holding hands, and the king said, "Oh no! The two of you are entwined with one another?"

The king was in such shock, he stumbled back and fell into his throne chair. He rested his head on his hand and said, "Son, what have you done?"

"Father, listen to me. Princess Ariel is not your enemy. She brings me the news of her father, King Philip knows we are coming tomorrow, it's an ambush. We must not attack."

King Ka'Ron lifted his head up and said, "Not my enemy, you say? But she is the intruder, is she not? Who killed four of my guards, and her father, King Philip, who wishes to end my life and rule my land, and now you are emotionally in love with my enemy's daughterm who is a *fucking* vampire? Forbidden love, the punishment of crossbreed is to be put to death. And when this war is over..." The king pointed his finger at Prince Kaiden and said, "You, re supposed to marry Princess Evelyn, King Richard's daughter." The king put his finger down and said, "The wedding ceremony has now been broken, he has the right to declare war on my *kingdom*! Now I have two enemies, your actions and choices have put me in stress. For the damage you have done, we're better off dying in that ambush tomorrow."

And then Kaiden said, "Father, I didn't mean to cause any of this."

"You have cost the kingdom of Galloway to be in danger, as your king. You must be put to death."

And then Lord Gerald quickly said, "Brother, wait! He is still your child."

King Ka'Ron looked at Lord Gerald and said, "Indeed he is," and the king looked back at Kaiden and said, "And for that. You must leave, you and the girl must never return. You are stripped of your title of prince."

Kaiden was displeased with what his father just told him, and Kaiden said, "But, Father!"

The king got very angry and said in a loud voice, "*Leave, boy! Fucking laeve!* Before I sic the damn guards on you!" The king stood up from his throne chair and pointed his finger at the door and said in an even loud voice, "*Get the fuck out!*"

Prince Kaiden and Princess Ariel immediately left the castle. As they were leaving, Ariel said to Kaiden, "I' am sorry," and he said to her, "Don't be, I got you."

When Lord Gerald and King Ka'Ron were now alone in the throne room, King Ka'Ron looked at Lord Gerald and said in a sorrow of pain, "What am I to do, brother? What am I to do when you and I both know what must be done now. Can you live with that?"

Lord Gerald responded and said, "I don't know, little brother. It's not always easy being king."

The king walked toward Lord Gerald and looked him in the eyes and said, "It must be done."

The king turned his back, and as he began to walk away, Lord Gerald approached the king from behind and laid his hand on the king's shoulder. He pulled out a long silver dagger and whispered in the king's ear and said, "Now you are aware of the ambush, little brother, it's no need to carry on with the original plan I had with King Philip, and I'll be damned if I allow you—"

Before the king had the chance to turn around, Lord Gerald stabbed the king in the back repeatedly. The king fell to the floor, and Lord Gerald lay on the floor with the king and held him. King Ka'Ron was slowly dying, and the king asked with a low voice and blood coming out of his mouth, "Why?"

As Lord Gerald held his little brother, he answered, "Why, you ask? I am your big brother, I've been living in your shadows, no more I say, living under your comfortability. I tried to kill you on the battlefield, but your son intervened. I've been planning this for years, carefully. No longer I wait, little brother. It's my time. *I reign!*"

And then Lord Gerald stabbed the king again for the final blow through the king's heart. Lord Gerald got up off the floor and cleaned the blood off the dagger. He looked around, and then he noticed someone was peeking through the other door. It was Princess Adrianna; she was watching the whole time.

Lord Gerald said, "Who's there?"

She was scared and backed up from the door, and Lord Gerald quickly rushed toward the door to see who was there. She saw him coming toward her; she was in fear, her heart pounding. She took off running. He burst open the door and saw Adrianna running down the hallway. He began to chase after her with the dagger in his hand and said, "Wait! Wait! It's not what you think."

She hid and tried to be quiet, and he said, "Adrianna. My niece, where are you?"

She said to herself, "I have to make it to my mom." She quietly and carefully came out of hiding and made her way toward her mom's room. The queen was in her room sound asleep. Adrianna burst through the door, shaking her mother out of her sleep, saying, "Mother! Mother! Get up, quit, get up."

The queen woke up in a panic and asked, "Honey, what's wrong?"

"Uncle Gerald killed Daddy."

"*What?*"

"It's true, Mother, you must believe me, now he's after me."

The queen got out of bed and started putting on decent clothes. Then the queen asked, "Where is your brother?"

"Father exiled him for being with Princess Ariel."

"Damn it! Go and get your sister, and the two of you grab a horse and find your brother."

"Yes, Mother, but what will you do?"

The queen walked toward the door, grabbed the doorknob, and before she opened the door, the queen said, "Go, I say, get your sister and find your brother. When I leave this room, you will wait here, and then leave after me. Do you understand?"

Adrianna said, "Yes, Mother."

The queen opened the door and walked down the hallway looking for Lord Gerald. She found him as he was still looking for Adrianna. She approached him from behind and said to him, "You don't have to look for her anymore, she came to me."

He turned around as he was surprised, and he said, "Hey, love."

And the queen said, "You killed my husband? Your own brother, for there is blood on you."

"Then you already know the answer."

The queen asked, "How could you, he is your flesh and blood?"

He answered in a yelling voice, "*How the fuck could I not*! *He* has taken everything from me…even you."

"Gerald, that was then, this is now."

He got upset and said, "I loved you first, before your father gave you away in marriage to my brother."

With tears in her eyes, she said, "And then you killed your brother and tried to kill my children."

The queen turned into a werewolf, then Lord Gerald dropped the dagger and turned into a werewolf as well. They began fighting and threw each other around, and as they were fighting, Adrianna made her way to Zy'Asiah's room, waking her up out of her sleep, saying, "Sis, get up! Sis, get up! *Get up!*"

And Zy'Asiah said in a very sleepy voice as she wished not to be bothered, "Ummm. Vampires up at night, werewolves sleep at night."

"We don't have time, we have to go!"

Zy'Asiah fully woke up and said, "What is it? Go where? And why are you so alarmed?"

Adrianna cried and said, "Father is dead! We must go now! Mother's orders."

"Okay, okay. Let's go."

## Meanwhile

Lord Gerald and Queen Lawanda were still fighting each other. He clawsed her across the chest, knocking her down to the ground. She turned back to normal, breathing for air. He approached her and stood over her as she bled, and she said, "Kill me like you killed my husband. My kids are safe and far."

The girls made it to the stable looking for a horse to steal. Zy'Asiah asked, "Where are we going?"

Adrianna answered, "We must find our brother."

Zy'Asiah said, "Brother most likely headed to cousin Shymair."

"And that is where we will go," Adrianna said.

Zy'Asiah asked, "What of Mother?"

"She told us to run and find our brother."

They grabbed two horses and got on. Suddenly, they heard guards yelling out, "The king and queen are dead! The king and queen are dead!"

One of the guards rang the big castle bell. A group of guards ran toward Adrianna and Zy'Asiah, yelling, "Stop! Stop at once!" They took off riding.

Lord Gerald was in his room, cleaning his brother's blood off him. As he did so, he sent for his consulting.

Minutes later, the consulting arrived, and he said, "Yes, my lord. You have summoned me?"

As Lord Gerald looked in the mirror, cleaning the blood off him, he asked, "Have the soldiers found my nephew and niece?"

The consulting answered, "No, my lord, the search still continues."

"That worries me. Send word to the assassin. Tell him I have work for him."

"As you wish, my lord. And what of King Philip's daughter?"

He turned around from the mirror, threw the bloody rag he used, and looked at him. He said, "Her father feels betrayed, he will deal with her."

"Of course, my lord."

*Meanwhile*

Kaiden and Ariel were on their horses, traveling, and he said to her, "We are outcasts, you and I, but I have no regrets because I have you."

She said, "Neither do I." He looked at her with a smile and said, "We will make a new life for ourselves far from here."

She asked, "Where will we go?"

He said, "Somewhere we can blend in, and no one will notice us. But in the meantime, we shall head to a place named the Wolf Clan Warrior. My cousin and his father are there. We can get ourselves together there."

She asked him, "Do you think your cousin will be kind to us, knowing that you are emotionally connected to a vampire?"

He said, "The one thing about a wolf pack, you follow your own damn rules."

"Then we shall ride."

They travel, heading east up the mountains.

## Meanwhile

Adrianna and Zy'Asiah were being chased by werewolf soldiers. They both ride as fast as they could, trying to get away. Zy'Asiah said, "They are gaining on us."

Adrianna said, "If we can't lose them, we fight them."

Zy'Asiah said, "It's five of them, the odds are against us."

Then Adrianna said, "Then we shall make it even, follow my lead." She turned into a werewolf, and Zy'Asiah looked at her and does the same. Adrianna jumped off the horse high in the air, and Zy'Asiah followed. They hid in the trees, and the soldiers stopped and noticed they lost them. They got off their horses to pick up a track.

Adrianna ripped two big branches off from the tree and quickly sharpened them with her claws. Zy'Asiah ripped a branch off the tree and did the same. When the soldiers got closer, the girls jumped down from the tree. Adrianna stabbed two of them in the head, killing two of them. Zy'Asiah stabbed the other one in the head, killing the third one. Adrianna pulled the branch out of the soldier's head and threw the branch at the other soldier, piercing him in the shoulder. She quickly ran toward him, the werewolf soldier, and she swung a right and a left, and pulled the branch out of his shoulder, and shoved the branch through his mouth and came out the back of his head.

As Zy'Asiah was fighting with the werewolf soldier, Adrianna quickly approached him from behind and twisted his head around. Zy'Asiah and Adrianna turnd back to normal, and Adrianna said, "We must go before more come."

Zy'Asiah whistled for the horses and said, "We have to find somewhere safe for the night."

They get on the horses, and Adrianna said, "Come on, let's head in this direction to see if we can find a roof overhead." They rode off until they eventually find shelter.

An hour later, they found shelter, and they got off their horses. Adrianna said, "This looks like a good place." It was an old, abandoned house, with broken windows hanging off. Cobwebs were everywhere. They went inside, and Zy'Asiah looked around the abandoned house and said, "It's a piece of shit."

Adrianna said, "It's only for tonight." They tried to get comfortable, and Adrianna started a fire in the hearth.

Zy'Asiah looked out the window and saw a rabbit. She said, "Ummm, delicious. I shall return."

Adrianna said, "Hurry back."

"Yeah, yeah. Pipe down, big sis. I am getting us food."

Zy'Asiah hunted and captured the rabbit then returned to the old, abandoned house and said, "See, I wasn't gone long." She handed the rabbit to her sister and said, "I hunted. You cook." Adrianna grabbed the rabbit, skinned it, gutted it, and cooked it.

Then they ate, and Zy'Asiah said, "That rabbit was good, I was hungry."

Adrianna said, "Me too."

Then Zy'Asiah was quiet for a moment, and then she said, "Wait, wait." Zy'Asiah looked at Adrianna, and Zy'Asiah said, "Oh, my."

Adrianna was concerned and said, "What's wrong?"

She said, "I just realized Mother and Father are gone, and our uncle is the cause of their deaths." Zy'Asiah's tears rolled down her face, and she said, "And we can't find our brother."

Adrianna got up, walked toward her, held her, and said, "Everything's going to be right, sis."

Zy'Asiah said, "Why would Father have our brother be exiled?"

As Adrianna held her, she said, "I am sure Father had his reasons. But we will find our brother, as Mother wished, and bring justice to our parent's death and restore order in the kingdom of Galloway through Kaiden."

Zy'Asiah looked at her and said, "I believe you."

Adrianna kissed her on the forehead and said, "Good. We will leave in the morning, we will head up east in the mountains. We will start there looking for our brother."

"Okay, let's try to get some sleep," Zy'Asiah said.

*Meanwhile hours later, before the sun came up*

Kaiden and Ariel finally arrived at their location, up east in the mountains at the Wolf Clan Warrior. They approached a big brown wooden gate. The man in the lookout tower said, "What's your business here?"

Kaiden yelled out, "I am Prince Kaiden with Princess Ariel. I'm here for General Shummy and Shymair!"

"Wait there!"

Minutes later, the lookout man returned and yelled out, "Open the gate, let them through!"

They entered the community of the Wolf Clan Warrior, and Ariel said, "I'm glad we made it. The sun is coming up soon, I can feel myself getting warm."

He looked at her and said, "I will find you shelter."

Kaiden saw Shymair coming toward them. Ariel and Kaiden dismounted from their horses, and Kaiden and Shymair happily approached each other with open arms. "Cousin, so good to see you," Shymair said.

They embraced each other with a big hug, and Kaiden said, "Glad to see you, cousin."

Shymair said, "Now, what brings you here?"

"It's a long story. I will share with you very soon," then Kaiden said, "Cousin, I would like to introduce you to Ariel." They both looked at her, and Kaiden said, "My lover."

Shymair looked surprised and said, "She's a vampire." He shook her hand and said, "Nice to meet you."

She said, "Nice to meet you as well."

Shymair said to her, "Vampires are welcome here in my community."

Kaiden said, "Thank you, cousin. She needs shelter before the sun comes up."

"Yes, of course. Follow me. My guards will tend to your horse."

As they followed Shymair, he asked her, "Have you fed?"

She answered, "No, but I'll be all right."

Shymair looked back at her, walked backward, and said, "No worries, we have blood here for our vampire visitors. The humans donate their blood, and in return, we give them food or make them weapons."

She said, "Thank you."

He turned back around and said, "Welcome."

Then they approached a shack house. Shymair opened the door and said, "Come. You can take shelter here."

They entered inside, and Shymair said, "I'll give you two some privacy." Shymair looked at Kaiden and said, "Cousin, we'll talk later." Then Shymair said to Ariel, "And we'll have someone bring you food."

As Shymair closed the door, Kaiden said, "Thank you very much."

He smiled and closed the door. Kaiden and Ariel got comfortable and settled in. There was a knock at the door. Kaiden opened the door, and it was someone from the community holding Ariel's food. "For the guest."

He grabbed the food and said, "Thanks," and closed the door. He walked toward Ariel and said, "My love." She grabbed it from him and drank the blood. Her eyes turned red as she was drinking, and some of the blood dripped down on the side of her lip. When she finished drinking the whole thing, she said, "That was good."

Her eyes turned back to normal, and Kaiden said as he wiped the blood off the side of her lip, "You are so sexy."

She said, "Well, get over here and show me how sexy I am."

They took each other's clothes off, lay down in bed, and made love.

Moments later, the sun came out, and Arianna and Zy'Asiah woke up that morning, got themselves together, and headed out.

# Chapter 7

# A New King

*Later that day*

At Galloway Castle, Lord Gerld was in the throne hall, sitting in the throne chair, imagining himself as king, already feeling proud. He said to his consulting, "The moment is near, it's finally coming," and the consulting, standing next to him, replied, "It's been a long time coming, my lord."

"Yes, it has. So many sacrifices I have made. What is rightfully mine is now rightfully mine." Lord Gerald then looked away, feeling a little mournful, and said, "But I had to spill family blood to get here." Lord Gerald looked back and said, "In a week, the council will announce me as the new king of Galloway."

In the middle of their conversation, a needle pierces the consulting's neck. He passed out and hit the floor. Lord Gerald looked up toward his right and saw the assassin emerge from the shadows.

He said to the assassin, "You are surprising, and yet I have some questions about you, but will get no answers. And I'm assuming the black leather clothes you are wearing from head to toe are protecting you from the sun, not too many vampires know that magic trick yet. If they stop depending on their familiars, like fetch dogs…they would have already figured that out. So that tells me you don't have a familiar. Now that's one thing I know about you."

The assassin said, "That will be the only thing you know about, for your life, keep it that way. Now I received your letter."

"Yes, I require your skills, people I need you to kill." Lord Gerald pulled out a list and handed it to the assassin. The assassin grabbed the list and looked it over. Lord Gerald said, "Details are revealed in the list."

The assassin noticed one name on the list, looked up, and said, "Trying to avoid paying your debt, I see."

"Find my nephew, you know what to do."

Then the assassin disappeared in the blink of an eye.

Up in the east mountains at the Wolf Clan Warrior, kids were playing outside, running around. Women were washing clothes by the lake and hanging them up to dry. Birds were flying and chirping in the trees. Ariel and Kaiden were sleeping, but Kaiden woke up first. He got up out of bed, put on his clothes, and splashed his face with water. Before he walked out the door, he looked at Ariel, who was still sleeping, and smiled at her. He opened the door and walked out, off the porch, and saw his cousin Shymair and others sitting by the firepit, drinking and eating.

Shymair yelled, "Cousin, come join us!"

When Kaiden sat down with the others, he said to Shymair, "Cousin, I would like to speak with you."

Shymair put down his cup and said, "Yes, of course." Then he said out loud, "Everyone! Give us some privacy!"

They get up and leave, and Shymair said, "So, tell me, cousin, what happened?"

Kaiden looked at him and said, "My father exiled me for being with a vampire. Ariel…Princess Ariel, King Philip's daughter, he almost killed her when he found us out."

"I'm sorry," Shymair said. "Where are the both of you heading?"

Kaiden answered, "South, by the Kingdom of Bridgeton. We will be on the outside, keeping to ourselves."

Shymair said, "King Albert B. Kelly is the king of the Kingdom of Bridgeton. Humans do not take kindly to us there. Be safe, my cousin. It's dangerous for us night creatures. And know there's always a home for the both of you here."

Kaiden looked at Shymair and said, "Thank you."

Shymair was quiet for a few seconds and then said, "I'm sorry I missed the passing of Jessica. I'm grateful you were there when she needed you, if only I could have been."

"She asked for you, she loved you. She's forever in our hearts."

Shymair tried not to cry, looked away, and wiped the tears from his eyes.

## Suddenly

The big brown wooden gate doors opened, and General Shummy and his wolf pack returned from hunting, carrying on their backs a deer and hogs. Shummy yelled, "*Nephew! Is that you?*"

Shymair, as his father was approaching them with the deer on his back, said, "Father, let me get that off you." Shymair grabbed the deer off his father's back, and Shummy said, "We will eat well tonight." Then Shummy said, "Nephew, I'm glad to see you."

Kaiden said, "I need your help."

"Anything you need," Shummy said.

Kaiden said, "Food, water, traveling equipment, and a house buggy with covered windows."

"Ummm, I will have what you require before the end of the day." Then Shummy asked, "Is everything all right at home?"

Kaiden looked away and said, "I have no home."

Shummy asked, "Do not tell me the Kingdom of Galloway has fallen?"

"No, the kingdom still stands tall."

"Then why the traveling equipment?"

"I am an outcast."

Shummy placed his hand on Kaiden's shoulder and said, "You must go in peace and be one with nature in the name of Yeshua." Then Shummy asked, "Are you traveling alone?"

"No, Ariel."

"Princess Ariel? King Philip's daughter?"

"Yes."

"And this is your reason for being outcast? Nephew, your home is here. I understand the werewolf in a man must make his own way."

95

"Thank you, Uncle Shummy."

When they were done with the conversation, Kaiden returned to the shack house. He walked inside, and Ariel was just waking up. He said, "Love, did you sleep well?"

"I sure did, my love."

Kaiden sat down at the table and then said, "We will be leaving soon, with everything we need."

"That's wonderful." She got up, washed her face, approached him, and sat next to him at the table. She said, "I wonder what our fathers are doing?"

"I don't know. They made their choice, and we made ours."

"Agreed."

General Shummy was done gathering everything Kaiden and Ariel needed for their journey. He knocked on their door and said, "Nephew!"

Kaiden opened the door and said, "Hey, Uncle."

"I have everything you need, nephew. You and your companion may leave when ready."

Shummy had prepared them a house buggy with covered windows, food, and supplies. Kaiden said, "Thank you."

"Anytime, nephew. Y'all take care of each other." They embraced each other with a hug, and then Shummy walked off the porch.

Kaiden closed the door and said to Ariel, "Are you ready to go, my love?"

She said, "Yes."

He grabbed the blanket off the bed and covered her to protect her from the sun. They quietly left the shack so Ariel could get inside the horse buggy. When they arrived, Kaiden got Ariel inside the horse buggy and closed the door behind her. Then he climbed on top of the house buggy and rode toward the gates.

Suddenly, Kaiden heard, "Wait! Wait!" His cousin Shymair yelled out as he rushed toward them. "Wait!" he yelled out again when he was near. He said, "My father almost forgot to give you this, for Ariel."

It was a jar of human blood Shymair handed him, and Kaiden said, "Thank you, cousin, she will need this."

Kaiden covered the jar, and Shymair said, "You weren't going to leave without saying goodbye now?"

He said, "'Course not." Kaiden dismounted from the house buggy.

They hugged each other tightly, and Shymair said, "Have a safe journey. I love you, cousin."

Kaiden said, "I love you more."

He got back on top of the house buggy, and Shymair yelled out, "Open the gates!"

They rode off, traveling on the path heading south of the Kingdom of Bridgeton. As they were traveling, Kaiden quickly opened the buggy door and handed the jar to Ariel, saying, "Thank you, right on time." He said, "We have a long way to go, my love, get comfortable," and she replied, "After I drink some of this, another nap will do me just fine."

## The day was now night

Adrianna and Zy'Asiah finally arrived at the Wolf Clan Warrior.

"Who is at the gate at this hour?" the man in the lookout tower asked.

"It is I, Princess Adrianna, and Princess Zy'Asiah. Our business here is with General Shummy, my uncle."

"Open the gates!"

When they entered through the gates, Shummy, Shymair, and the others were all sitting by the firepit. Shummy stood up from the log he was sitting on when he saw them coming in, and he said, "Adri and Zy, what a surprise to see you both."

They dismounted from their horses and rushed toward Uncle Shummy with open arms, tears flying out of their eyes, and they embraced him with a hug.

"Hey, hey. Is everything all right?" he asked.

As they were both hugging him, Adrianna said in a stressed voice, "Mother and Father are dead."

Shymair was shocked by what he just heard and said, "What's this now?" Shummy stepped back and looked at them and said, "What is it you speak of?"

With the stress on Zy'Asiah's face and the sadness in her voice, she said, "It's true, Uncle Shummy. Our father and mother have been murdered by the hands of our uncle Gerald."

"Lord Gerald?" Shummy said in disbelief.

"*What!*" Shymair yelled.

"Oh, in the name of Yeshua, Kaiden does not know of this," Shummy said.

"We are looking for our brother," Zy'Asiah said.

Shymair said, "He was here, he left this morning."

"Where has he gone?" Adrianna asked.

"East, to the outside of the Kingdom of Bridgeton," Shymair answered.

And Adrianna said, "He is a day ahead of us."

"Why Bridgeton?" Adrianna asked.

"Easy for him to blend in with the humans," Shummy answered.

"Bridgeton is a four-day journey, is it not?" Zy'Asiah asked.

"Yes, it is. We shall go to find our brother as Mother wished," Adrianna said.

"I'll gather all your supplies and everything you need for travels in the morning. Stay with us until then," Shummy said.

The girls hugged him and said, "Thank you," and he replied, "Yes, and I have to go and tell my wife about her sister. She just got back with her group." Then Shummy said, "You girls can sleep in the guest house shack."

He looked at Shymair and said, "Son, show your cousins where they can lay their heads and put their horses up."

"Yes, Father. Y'all come with me."

But little did they know, the assassin was hiding in a tree, listening to the whole conversation. He had followed Adrianna and Zy'Asiah after he spoke with Lord Gerald. He was able to pick up their tracks when the girls killed those werewolf soldiers. Then the trail led him to the banded house where the girls slept, and the assassin continued to follow more of their tracks to the Wolf Clan Warrior.

The assassin telepathed to his hawk named Huffy, saying, "Come to me." They had a special blood bond; the assassin and Huffy could see through each other's eyes and teleport to each other. Huffy flew in the air, circling around them, and then teleported onto the assassin's shoulder. He gave Huffy a treat and said, "Huffy, follow the girls while I take care of business in the Kingdom of Cumberland."

Huffy did so, and the assassin jumped down from the tree and left.

## Time had passed, it was now morning

Adrianna and Zy'Asiah woke up from their sleep, yawning and stretching. When they were done getting themselves together, they came outside and saw Uncle Shummy had everything ready for their travels.

They approached him, and Adrianna said, "Thank you for doing this," and Zy'Asiah said, "Awesome, Uncle."

Then Kim came out of her house, filled with emotions for the loss of her sister, Lawanda, and her brother-in-law. She approached the girls, saying, "Girls, I'm so glad to see you both. When I heard the news, I wanted to give you girls sometime to breathe. I can't believe this happened to your mother and father. The pain hurts deep for my sister."

Zy'Asiah said, as she tried not to cry, "It's a very painful loss."

And Kim said, "And by the hands of your uncle, this is tragic."

Adrianna said, "And now we must find our brother."

"He was just here, and I missed him when I returned. I hope he's doing all right," Kim said, feeling worried.

They hugged, and Kim said as she was crying, "Please be safe and come back safe."

"We will, Auntie," they both said.

Adrianna said to Uncle Shummy as he was approaching, his wife wiping her tears from her eyes and holding her, "Thank you for doing this."

And he said, "Your brother said the same thing to me before he left... I have faith you will find him."

"I have faith too."

Then Kim said, "I feel more comfortable if your cousin rides along with y'all," and Shymair quickly said, "Yes, I would love to come."

Zy'Asiah said, "Of course. Please come with us."

Adrianna climbed on the back of the horse-drawn wagon, Zy'Asiah climbed back there with her, and Shymair climbed up front of the horse-drawn wagon to steer the horses. Shummy and Kim walked beside the horse-drawn wagon toward the big brown gates.

When they got close, Shummy yelled out, "Open the gates!" then he looked at them and said, "Y'all get back safe, and may Yeshua be with you," and Shymair said, "See you soon, Father and Mother."

Then Kim yelled out as they were riding through the gates, "Come back soon!"

Shymair stood up and turned around and said, "Love you both!" Zy'Asiah and Adrianna waved. And they headed out on the pathway, traveling to the kingdom of Bridgeton to find Kaiden.

Huffy flew and followed them. "Let the journey begin," the assassin said, seeing through Huffy's eyes as he was still traveling to Cumberland.

Hours later and with four hours left of daylight, the assassin, with black leather from head to toe to protect him from the sun, arrived in the land of Cumberland. He sneaked into the castle quietly, moving in the shadows. He saw his mark, King Philip, resting in bed with his queen, Helen. The assassin approached the king very quietly, pulled out a wooden sharp stake, and stabbed him through the heart. King Philip woke up, surprised, and saw his killer, saying, "You!" The king turned into fire and burned, and then the queen woke up from a deep sleep, disoriented and confused.

"What's this!" she said in a loud panic. The assassin moved into the shadows and disappeared like a ghost. The queen screamed. The bed was a pile of ash, and the king's crown lay on the burnt pillow. The guards heard the queen scream and rushed to the king's bedroom chambers. When they arrived, the guards saw the pile of ash on the bed, and one of the guards said, "The king has been assassinated!"

The assassin left the land of Cumberland and sent a messenger pigeon to Lord Gerald with a tiny note attached to its leg. Lord Gerald was in his room, sitting at his desk, reading books on politics. The pigeon landed on the windowsill. He removed the note from the pigeon's leg, and it read, "King Philip is dead."

He smiled and crumbled the tiny note and said to the guard who was standing outside his door, "Guard! Send for my consulting."

The consulting arrived at Lord Gerald's room, and he said, "You have summoned me, my lord?"

Lord Gerald looked at him and said, "King Philip is no longer a concern."

"Excellent, my lord."

Then Lord Gerald said so proudly, "Nothing is getting in my way," and then he said with a happy smirk, "And tomorrow, they are announcing me as the new king of Galloway."

"You will make a good king," the consulting said with his hands folded behind his back.

Lord Gerald stood from his chair, walked toward him, and said, "When the second person on that list is no longer breathing air, we can move forward with our plan, and I can finally get back every silver and gold I spent just getting to this moment. The kingdom of Galloway will be even more powerful."

"Indeed, we will be, my lord."

*Moments later*

The assassin traveled to the kingdom of Vineland, the land of humans. King Booker and his wife, Queen Hannah, were the royalty of the kingdom of Vineland. The assassin patiently waited to strike at midnight, so he hid in a banded barn house where he rested until then.

The time had come for the assassin to move out. He sneaked into the castle like a shadowy ghost. King Booker was in his bedroom chambers having sex with his queen, Hannah. The assassin shadowed under the king's door and hid under their bed like a boogeyman. When they were done making love and lying in bed together, they looked at each other, and the king said, "I love you, baby," and the queen said, "And I love—"

The assassin came out from under the bed fast and pulled a knife out, cutting the king's throat. Before the queen even had the chance to scream or finish her sentence, the assassin knocked her out and placed the knife in her hands. He opened the door and yelled out down the halls, "Guards! Guards! The queen has killed the king!"

The guards burst through the door. The assassin hid in the shadows. The guards saw the king lying in bed in a puddle of blood with a knife in the hands of the wife. They woke her up, and she said, "No. I didn't do this. *Nooo!* I swear," and they arrested her.

The assassin made his way out of Vineland and found a place that was comfortable for him in the woods by the lake that reminded him of back home in Salem. He sat on a rock, writing a little note. He opened his messenger pigeon cage, tied the little note to the pigeon's leg, and sent the messenger pigeon to Lord Gerald. The pigeon arrived in Galloway in the morning.

Today was the day they announced Lord Gerald as the new king of Galloway. He was getting a new set of clothes and stood on the stool with arms open as the tailor measured his arms and legs. The pigeon tapped at the window. The consulting opened the window, grabbed the pigeon, and removed the little note from the pigeon's leg. He let the pigeon go, and it flew off. The consulting showed Lord Gerald the note, and it read, "King Booker is dead."

He smiled at his consulting and said, "Marvelous."

*Moments later*

Thousands of Galloway people came to see their new king, Lord Gerald, on a high balcony and stood high and proud as they announced him to be the new king. The crown was placed on his head, and then they played the trumpet. He waved to the people.

# Chapter 8

# Search for the True King

*Weeks later*

In the Kingdom of Bridgeton, the sky was gray and cloudy, the clouds blocking the sun, and the weather was cold, with snowflakes falling to the ground. The snow was a foot deep. Kaiden and Ariel were traveling through the snow. She looked out of the horse buggy window, saw people walking along the side of the pathway bundled up and carrying their belongings. She said, "So this is Bridgeton."

They traveled farther out of the community, to the outskirts of the kingdom of Bridgeton, to keep a low profile. They came across an open field, and Kaiden said, "Whoa!" as he pulled back the snaffle rein for the horses to stop. Kaiden dismounted from the horse buggy, opened the door for Ariel, and she stepped down to look at the open field. Kaiden asked her, "What do you think, my love? It's far out and away from people. If it doesn't please you, baby, we can keep looking."

She looked at him and said, "You're always trying to please me, love." She smiled and then said, "But no, baby, it's perfect. Let's get started."

Kaiden used his werewolf strength to claw down trees, and Ariel did the same using her vampire strength. They carried two huge logs on their shoulders. A civilian wino who could barely stand, holding a bottle in his hand, was walking by and saw them carrying the huge logs on their shoulders. The wino said, "What the fuck!" and his eyes got big. "I need to stop drinking, or maybe I need to drink more." The wino went on about his business, and they continue to build their house using common wire, long nails, a saw, and a hammer that Uncle Shummy supplied them on their travels.

Hours later, the house was complete. They settled in and sat on the floor with their backs against each other.

"How about tomorrow we get some furniture?" Ariel suggested.

He said, "Good idea. I could use a good bed."

And she said, "Me too, love."

He said, "This is the beginning of our new lives; it starts here."

"As long as we have each other."

## Meanwhile

Adrianna, cousin Shymair, and Zy'Asiah were still in pursuit of their search for Kaiden. Huffy soared over them. Shymair looked up and noticed a hawk flying over them, but he paid the hawk no mind.

Back at Galloway castle, King Gerald was having a meeting with his generals. They waited for their new king in the war room. The guard walked into the war room and announced the king's arrival, "All rise!"

The generals stood up from their chairs. The king walked into the war room and said, "Thank you all for coming, gentlemen. Take your seats. Let's get down to business." The generals sat down, and as the king was sitting down, he said, "I arranged this gathering for the interest of the Kingdom of Galloway. As we all know, King Booker is dead, and his wife is being charged with murder. Their kingdom is now vulnerable, they have no leader, no guidance, the head of the snake is cut off. But what does this have to do with us, before you ask." The king looked at them and said, "*Gold!*"

"Gold?" one of the generals asked.

The king said, "Yes, gold. And a lot of it. That shit Booker has a cave of gold. Don't know if the bastard was aware he was sitting on a gold mine. But I'm assuming if he did, I'm pretty sure he would have his workers mining the gold. But to ease your curiosity of how I came across these gold mines. My scouts came back and reported to me."

"What's the plan, my king?"

King Gerald answered, "We invade and conquer the kingdom of Vineland, under our law, and put those people to work in the gold mine. And use the gold to make our empire even more powerful!"

"Agreed."

"Agreed."

"Agreed."

The other general asked, "When do we start, my king?"

King Gerald got up from his chair and said, "Tomorrow."

The generals got up and left the war room, and the king's consulting spoke privately. The consulting said, "I see your plan will work, my king."

"Yes, this is why I had King Booker killed and his wife taking the fall for the crime. With her out of the way, that leaves no one for the throne, not even the kids."

"Indeed, the assassin proved himself well."

"Now let us get ready for tomorrow. It's a big day for the Kingdom of Galloway."

## The next day

At night, the moon was full, the stars bright, and the sky clear. One thousand werewolf soldiers howled at the moon as they stormed the kingdom of Vineland. They jumped on the castle walls, killing the guards, and the people yelled and screamed in terror, scared for their lives. The people of the city yelled out as they were covered in blood, limbs cut off, "May the bright light soldiers help us!"

The kingdom of Vineland was on fire, and blood was splattered everywhere. Many thousands of soldiers fought back with their swords, crossbows, and arrows, but sadly, they lost. The werewolves breached the castle's door and stormed their way in, killing more guards. Some of the guards had the courage to fight but lost. A few guards were in the throne hall with the door barricaded, and one guard said, "This is pointless! What are we even fighting for? We don't even have a king."

The werewolves busted the door down, and one guard said, "*No, no, no, no!*" as he was ripped limb from limb. Queen Hannah was locked up in the dungeon. She heard the commotion from within the castle and was terrified. She said, "First, my false accusation, and now werewolves are attacking. Have we angered Yahweh? Does the Kingdom of Vineland have hope?"

The words the queen had spoken was of a woman who was scared for her life and the lives of her people, and even though her people are accusing her of her husband's murder, she still held hope. Suddenly, she heard someone coming downstairs in the dungeon, and she said in tears, "Please! I beg of you. Whoever you are, please have mercy on my people."

The queen saw a werewolf approaching her closer, and the werewolf growled with saliva dripping down from the side of his mouth. Her pupils grew bigger, she trembled, her heart was pounding fast, she breathed heavily. The werewolf approached closer to the cell door. She begged for mercy.

The werewolf turned to normal, and it was King Gerald. He said to her, "Oh, I"m not going kill you. You did your part of you being accused of killing your husband." Then King Gerald smirked and said, "But I know the truth. I'm going to leave you in here to rot. Your kingdom is now mine."

She was too scared to speak. He walked away and left the dungeon. When the werewolf soldiers were done invading, most of them turned back to normal and gathered up the people they had spared from slaughter. King Gerald gave a speech, saying, "Humans of Vineland, you are now under the rule of the Kingdom of Galloway. If you wish to survive, you will do as you are told. I am your new king, and I have spoken!"

*The next day,*

King Gerald had the people working in the gold mine; they were slaves, working day in and day out, praying to Yahweh for their freedom. Some tried to escape but were punished, and the next day,

King Gerald felt generous enough just to feed Queen Hannah scraps of nasty food for the rest of her days.

## Six months later

In a small, poor village named Woodbine of humans. Unfortunately, because it's a poor village, vampires prey on the people of Woodbine at night. Because of this, most of the people of the village were not too friendly with strangers in their community. The village had residents of 220 people, and every other week, 1 went missing.

Adrianna, Zy'Asiah, and Shymair stopped at a tavern named the Bucket of Blood. They went inside, and everyone looked at them because the people of the village don't have too many strangers. After they closed the door behind them, Huffy, the assassin's hawk, landed on the roof of the tavern. They approached the bar, and the barkeep said to them, "We don't get too many strangers out here. What's your business?"

Zy'Asiah said, "We require good cooked meat."

Shymair said, "And beer!"

Adrianna said, "No beer for me and my sister, barkeep," and she handed the barkeep three coins. He took the coins and said, "Your business is good here. Take a seat over there, and I'll have someone bring your nourishment."

They sat down at the table, and Adrianna said, "I'm so hungry."

"We could have saved our coins and hunted for our food," Zy'Asiah suggested.

Shymair said, "As long as I'm getting my beer," then he saw his beer coming, happy and goofy as he could be, and he said, "Ahhh! I see our food coming now." The servant put the drinks down on the table and said, "Your food will be here soon." Shymair grabbed and chugged his drink down his throat, Zy'Asiah looked at him with big eyes as beer poured down the side of his face, and she said, "How can you drink that?"

"It's delicious," he said.

As they were still waiting for their food, five vampires were sitting in a dark corner on the other side of the tavern. The people of Woodbine never knew they were vampires. The five of them only show their vampire fangs when they have someone alone at night, terrified of their lives. They live in a cave far away. The five of them named themselves the Lost Boys. They watched Adrianna, Zy'Asiah, and Shymair, and the Lost Boys quietly whispered to each other. One of them said, "Filthy dogs, werewolves," and another one said, "We can rob them and take their goods."

Moments later, Adrianna, Zy'Asiah, and Shymair's food finally arrived. "Oh, good. The food is coming. I'm starving," Adrianna said. As they were eating their food, the Lost Boys left the tavern. When Shymair, Adrianna, and Zy'Asiah were done eating, they left a tip for the servant. "Nice and full," Adrianna said. They walked outside and headed toward the horse wagon.

"I feel better," Zy'Asiah said.

They got on the horse wagon, and Shymair said, "Time to get back to the search," and rode off. Huffy flew and followed. As they were traveling on the pathway, they came across a large log blocking the pathway.

"Whoa!" Shymair said, pulling back the snaffle rein to stop the horse.

"What's this?" Adrianna asked.

"Why is this log here?" Zy'Asiah asked.

Shymair said, "Keep your guard up. I'll take care of it." He dismounted from the horse wagon, approached the log, and picked the log up then threw it. Suddenly, the leader of the Lost Boys aimed a crossbow at the side of Shymair's head, and the leader said, "Don't move, werewolf." The other five quickly came out of hiding in a blink of an eye, surrounded the horse wagon, aiming their crossbows at the girls, and Shymair said, "Fucking vampires."

Then the leader said, "We are the Lost Boys. How about you girls come down from that wagon?" The girls got down from the wagon, and the leader said to Shymair, "This is how this is going to go. You're going to give us everything you and anything we ask. Give us a hard time, and this arrow will be going through your head."

Shymair's hands are up, and he asked, "May I turn around?"

"Don't try anything, dog."

Shymair turned around and said, "May I ask for your name?"

"David."

"Okay, David, I will make a deal with you. If you let us go with our belongings, I will be glad to make it worth more than your imagination. You don't have to rob people anymore. So you won't think I'm bullshitting, I will give you the location of my home, and you can wait for me there. When I return from my travels, do we have a deal?"

The other two vampires jumped on top of the wagon and started going through their belongings. David said, "Fuck that deal."

The assassin saw this situation through the eyes of Huffy. He realized that if something happened to them, he would lose his opportunity to find Prince Kaiden. The assassin telepathically communicated with Huffy and said, "Attack David."

Huffy attacked. "Get this damn bird off me! Now!"

They realized they had an opportunity to take advantage of the situation. Zy'Asiah and Adrianna nodded their heads at each other. They moved fast, took the vampires' crossbows, and kicked them so hard, they impacted the horse wagon, causing the other two vampires standing on top of the horse wagon to lose their balance and shoot the other two in the head. They burned into fire. As Huffy was attacking David, Shymair took his crossbow and kicked him. He fell to the ground, and before he had the chance to get back up, Shymair shot David in the shoulder. The assassin told Huffy to fly away. Adrianna and Zy'Asiah killed the other two vampires, stabbing them through the heart with arrows. They burned into fire. David was on the ground bleeding from his shoulder, and David said, "Come on, man. How about that deal, huh?"

Shymair said, "Fuck that deal," and turned into a werewolf. He ripped David apart from the waist, and he burned and turned into fire and ash.

## Meanwhile

In the outskirts of the Kingdom of Bridgeton, in the snowy weather, Kaiden and Ariel were enjoying their new lives. She was by the fire in a rocking chair, drinking a jar of human blood and reading a book, and Kaiden was outside chopping wood. He spotted a rabbit, threw his axe at it, and walked over to the dead rabbit, picked it up, and said, "Ummm. Lunch."

Then he skinned the dead rabbit, gutted it, and hung it up. Kaiden went back to continue chopping wood. When he was done chopping wood, he brought the wood inside along with the dead rabbit. Kaiden placed the wood by the fire and said, "Look, love, I have food for us to eat." He placed the dead rabbit on top of the fire to cook, and Ariel said, "Leave mine half-bloody, like how I like it."

He looked at her and said, "Love, I know what you like and don't like."

She smiled with a curious face and said, "And what is it that I don't like?"

"When I snore."

She laughed, "Hahahaha! You do snore loud."

As he had his back turned, she got up from the rocking chair and jumped on his back, and they wrestled. She put him in a leg lock and said, "Now beg for mercy."

He laughed and said, "I give, I give."

She released him, and as he was still lying on the floor, it seemed like he was helpless. She reached over to him and kissed him, and he said, "That gave me the strength to get up."

She sat on the bed, and he got up off the floor and said, "After we are done eating lunch, would you like to go for a walk? The sky is gray and cloudy."

"Of course, I would love to."

When the rabbit was done cooking, they ate, and they left for their walk. Eventually, they came across one of their favorite places to relax, a hot spring lake in the snow. They took their clothes off and went for a swim. "It's so warm," she said.

"I love this," he said.

## Moments later

When they were done swimming, they got out of the hot spring lake, put their clothes back on, and walked near a river fall. "It's beautiful here. I love coming here," she said.

Kaiden looked at her and said, "It's beautiful just like you. When I see this place, I think of you, because I see you."

She said, "I love you, and I am grateful for how you adore me. The love I see you have for me is priceless. The love I have for you is unexplainable." She looked deep into his eyes and said, "I would die for you, Kaiden."

He looked deep into her eyes and said, "And I would die for you, Ariel."

They grabbed each other's hands and walked back home in the snow. Finally, they made it home. Kaiden started a fire, and Ariel undressed to get into something more comfortable. He watched her change her clothes, like a horny dog. When she was done changing, she sat down in her rocking chair and continued to read her book. She raised her eyes up and noticed Kaiden was changing his clothes. She watched him, like a horny bat, and said, "Oh my." When he was done changing his clothes, he added more wood to the fire.

Moments later, Kaiden and Ariel lay in bed, holding each other, and they talked for hours until they fell asleep.

## The next day

"It's not too far from now we are about to enter the Kingdom of Bridgeton," Adrianna said.

"I just hope we don't get attacked no more," Zy'Asiah said.

And then Shymair said, "I'm still trying to figure out where that hawk came from." He was confused. "Why did it help us? It looks like the same hawk that's been following us." Then he looked up to the sky and said, "But I don't see it around now."

Moments later, they finally arrived in the Kingdom of Bridgeton. The city of the community had a bakery named Doughboy that made delicious cakes. You could hear the Catholic church bells ringing, the Bright Light soldiers patrolling the streets, kids running around playing, and a homeless man standing in front of the clothing store begging for money. Adrianna, Shymair, and Zy'Asiah got down from the horse wagon. "My cousin Kaiden is here somewhere, and we shall find him."

Adrianna said, as she was the more responsible one, "Now remember, let us tread carefully and blend in. We are simply looking for our brother." She looked at Shymair and said, "Find us somewhere to stay for tonight, Zy and I will ask around for Kaiden."

He said, "You got it," as he walked off.

The girls walked around the city, describing to people what Kaiden looked like and asking if they had seen him. Everyone said, "No."

Huffy flew around the city, looking for Kaiden. Two hours later, Shymair returned to the girls, and he said, "Any word of my cousin yet?"

"No, nothing," Adrianna answered.

"We asked for hours," Zy'Asiah said.

And Shymair said in a frustrated voice, "Damn! I was hoping for something."

"Did you find us a place to stay?" Adrianna asked.

"Yes, I got us a room for rent."

"Good, let's settle in, and we can try in the morning. He's here somewhere," Adrianna said.

And Shymair said, "Okay, follow me."

Huffy followed them, soaring in the air. They arrived at the room, and Huffy landed on the roof and watched them walk inside. They went into their room and got comfortable. Huffy flew off to a barn, flew inside the barn, and the assassin teleported through Huffy. He rubbed Huffy's head and said, "Good boy." The assassin put food out for Huffy to eat. Huffy got comfortable and lay down on the hay.

Meanwhile, Shymair and the girls were lying down on the bed. Shymair said, "Hope we find Kaiden tomorrow."

"Me too," Adrianna said. Zy'Asiah was already asleep.

"Good night," they both said.

The assassin stayed in for the night at the barn.

Five days they searched for the true king. On day 6, Shymair and the girls got up in the morning and decided to go to the tavern named the Oak. When they got there, they ordered food and drinks and asked the people in the tavern about Kaiden, describing what he looked like. One person said, "Yes, I have seen who you are describing. He came into my shop buying furniture. I remember him and his lover. They moved out there into that open field and built their new house."

And then the wino, who was always drunk, jumped into the conversation and said out loud, "And I saw them build it."

"Are you sure?" Adrianna asked.

"Sure, as I am drunk." The wino hiccupped and then said, "I have seen some strange things in my life." The wino drank more of his wine and said, "But I have never seen a man and woman carry two big logs on their shoulders." The wino drank more of his wine and said, "Not enough alcohol for that." The wino drank his last sip of wine, holding his wine jar over his head with his tongue out trying to get the last drop. Then he said, "Oh, no." Out of the goods, the wino got an idea and said, "Let's make a deal." The wino hiccupped and said, "Give me coin for more wine, and I'll show you where I saw who you are looking for."

Zy'Asiah whispered in Adrianna's ear and said, "Can we trust him? He is a drunk."

She whispered back and said, "He's our only lead."

Shymair said, "Deal!"

The wino jumped up and down with joy and said, "Haha, let's go!"

They left the tavern and headed toward their horse wagon. Shymair climbed up to steer the horses, the girls and the wino climbed on the back of the wagon. "*Let's go!*" Shymair yelled out. they take off, and Huffy followed them.

Moments later, they finally made it to the open field and saw the wooded house the wino man was talking about. The wino rubbed his hands together as he was happy with joy, and he said, "I can almost taste my coin."

And Shymair said, "And taste that liquor soon too."

As they were approaching the wooden house, Kaiden was inside at the table eating fruits; Ariel was reading her book. Kaiden said to her calmly with his head down, "Love."

She looked up from her book and said, "Yes?"

And he said, "I hear someone coming." Kaiden looked up at her and then said, "Don't know if they are friends or foes, but let us be cautious."

They both got up, and she grabbed her two wrist blades, and her eyes turned red. Shymair, the girls, and the wino approached the wooden house closer. They got down from the horse wagon, and Ariel walked toward the window. She slowly moved the curtain to peek through the window and said, "I see two girls and a man," then she looked at Kaiden and said, confused, "And they're with that guy that's always drinking."

Shymair, the girls, and the wino were getting closer to the wooden house. Kaiden said, "My fangs aren't tingling, no threat," then Kaiden sniffed with his nose and said, "But that smell is familiar." He walked toward the window and said, "Let me have a look." He peered through the window and said, "In the name of Yeshua." He was happy to see who the unknown guests were.

"Who is it?" Ariel asked.

He looked at her and said, "Come outside with me and see."

Ariel and Kaiden went outside, and the girls and Shymair saw Kaiden coming outside. They were so excited, they ran toward each other and embraced one another with hugs. Zy'Asiah was crying with joy as she hugged her little brother Kaiden, and she said, "I missed you so much."

"I missed you," Kaiden said.

"We finally found you, little brother," Adrianna said as she hugged him.

When they were done hugging each other, Kaiden asked them, "What are you guys doing out here?"

"It's best if we talked inside," Adrianna said.

And Shymair said, "Yes, it's very important what your sisters have to tell you, cousin."

Kaiden was concerned and asked, "You guys look worried, is everything all right?"

Then Zy'Asiah said, "Please, brother, let us speak inside."

"Okay then, let us go in," Kaiden said.

Before they walked off, the wino man was covering his mouth with a tight fist, clearing his throat to get their attention as they forgot to pay him, and he said, "Forgetting something?"

Kaiden said to the wino man, "Oh you're welcome in too."

"Oh, brother, he is not with us," Adrianna said. Then she looked at Shymair; he paid the wino. "Well, all right, back to the Oak I go. See you guys around," the wino jolly-walked off.

As they were heading back inside, Kaiden said, "With the excitement, I almost forgot." He looked at Ariel and said, "My love, please forgive me." Then he looked at his sisters and said, "This beautiful woman is Ariel, the love of my life. Ariel, these two lovely ladies are my big sisters. Adrianna is the firstborn, Zy'Asiah is the second born."

Zy'Asiah looked at Ariel and noticed her eyes and said, "You're a vampire."

Ariel's eyes turned back to normal, and Ariel said, "Yes, I am."

They were almost closer to the house, and Zy'Asiah reached her hand out toward Ariel. Ariel grabbed her hand, and they shook hands. Then Zy'Asiah said, "Well then, it is a pleasure to meet you, vampire Ariel."

"Oh no, the pleasure is mine."

Then Adrianna said, "I can see my brother loves you and you love him." Adrianna opened her arms and said to Ariel, "Come, hug. They hugged, and Adrianna said, "You are family now, vampire or not."

"Thank you very much, I needed that."

Then Shymair joined in on their hug and said, "I'm happy we're all together again."

They walked inside the house, and Huffy landed on top of the roof. When they got inside, Kaiden walked toward the hearth to burn more wood to warm the house. The house got cold when they left the door open. Shymair sat in the chair, Zy'Asiah sat in Ariel's rocking chair, Ariel sat on their bed, and Adrianna sat at the table. She said to Kaiden, "Brother, please, sit with me. I must tell you something disturbing to hear of Father and Mother." You could hear the sadness in her voice.

Kaiden sat down at the table and said, "What of Father and Mother?"

Adrianna tried not to cry and struggled with the words to say. "Mother and father…are dead."

Ariel was surprisingly shocked by this news, she swallowed a breath of air, covered her mouth with her hands, and said, "Oh dear Yeshua."

Kaiden stood up from the chair as he was troubled by this and in disbelief. He said in a strong tone of voice, "What is this you speak of?"

Zy'Asiah was emotional and said, "Our sister speaks the truth, brother."

He was angry and asked them, "By whose hands, who spilled my parents' blood?" Kaiden got more upset and looked up to the heavens, with his hand raised up and said in a deep werewolf voice, "I shall curse their name, and my parents will be avenged in my veins."

Zy'Asiah got up from the bed and placed her hand on Kaiden's shoulder and said, "It was Uncle Gerald who killed our father and mother."

As he looked at her, he said, "No! He would never."

"Brother, please. It's the truth, I saw him kill Father with my own eyes and try to kill me when I witnessed the murder. Uncle Gerald stole the crown, killed our parents, and drove you away," Arianna said.

Before Shymair spoke, Zy'Asiah sat back down in the rocking chair, and Shymair said, "This is why we are here, out looking for you."

Kaiden looked at them and slowly sat back down in the chair and said, "This is disturbing news."

Then Shymair said, "Cousin, it's time to go back, fight back, and take back what is rightfully yours. And uphold your family's name, restore the Kingdom of Gallway of the true king. I will fight with you to the bloody end."

"He is right, my love, you must go back. And I'm with you," Ariel said.

Kaiden looked at them and said, "Gerald is no longer our uncle, he is our enemy, the snake in the grass he is, the devil himself. There is no honor in a man killing his own brother for whatever reason. The curse of Cain killing Abel lives on. My mother and father will have their vengeance, I will strike this fallen angel morning star down, with my own hands, with a sword, and then he can have his last words...with me!"

"I'm with you," Zy'Asiah said.

"And I'm with you, brother," Adrianna said.

"Baby, I will walk through the gates of hell with you, I'm with you," Ariel said.

"Cousin, you have always had my loyalty. The Wolf Clan stands with you."

And then Kaiden said, "Then we shall in the morning."

## Moments later, the hour was midnight

Shymair and the girls settled in and made themselves comfortable by laying out pillows and blankets to sleep on the floor, near the fire because it was warmer. Ariel was back in her rocking chair, reading her book, while Kaiden lay in bed. He said, "We should try to get some rest, the morning awaits us."

"I could use some shut-eye," Ariel said as she closed her book, got up from the rocking chair, and headed toward the bed to lie down with her lover.

"Good night, brother, cousin, and Ariel," Adrianna said. Zy'Asiah said the same.

"Good night, family," Kaiden said.

When they ended their night, Huffy flew off the roof and into the woods, landing on a branch. The assassin teleported through Huffy, saying, "Good boy," as he made camp and watched them in the house from a distance. He sat by the fire, fed Huffy fish, and said to his companion, "So, my little friend, tell me what you know."

Huffy telepathically conveyed the conversation he had heard in the house, and the assassin said, "Well then, let us end the night, and we will follow them in the morning."

# Chapter 9

# The Prince Comes Home

It's a new day. The morning was here, the sky was gray and cloudy, blocking the sun. Kaiden was the first one up in the morning, and soon everyone else got up, stretching and yawning. They washed their faces with water, and Adrianna said, "Let us have a good meal before we leave. We have a long way back home."

"I agree," Shymair said.

Zy'Asiah suggested, "Let's eat at the Oak, they have good food there."

"Ummm, they do have good bloody steak," Ariel said. And then Zy' Asiah noticed Kaiden wasn't present in the house and she said, "Hey, wait! Where's brother?"

"He's outside, getting the horses and wagon and the horse buggy together," Shymair answered.

As Kaiden was preparing the horses and wagon, strapping down the gear, the assassin watched him like a lion stalking its prey, patiently waiting for the right moment to strike. "I am going outside and help Kaiden. The fast we get done, the faster we can go to the Oak," Ariel said as she was walking out the door, Kaiden saw her coming outside. She was standing by the door; he smiled at her and said, "Hello, my love."

Before she even walked off the steps, Kaiden's fangs tingled of threat nearby. He looked concerned and stopped what he was doing, sniffing to get a whiff of the direction of the threat was coming from. Suddenly, his werewolf ears heard a whistle of flying needle heading toward him, and he quickly caught the needle in a blink of an eye with his two fingers and said, "What the hell?"

Ariel had a confused look on her face. Shymair and the girls came outside behind her. Kaiden stared at the needle, and then he realized they were being attacked and yelled out, "Back inside! Now!"

Then dozens of flying needles came out of the woods. One needle pierced Adrianna in the shoulder; she felt faint and drowsiness, slowed breathing, and dizzy. She lost her balance and fell to the floor. Shymair grabbed her before she fell to the floor completely, and he dragged her inside the house.

Kaiden tried to catch a few of the needles so they could have a chance to take cover. Ariel and Zy'Asiah ducked for cover behind the wagon. The assassin ran out of the woods and into the open field. He jumped sixty feet in the air, like a soaring bat. As he was in the air, he quickly reached from his waist to grab smoke bombs and threw smoke bombs at them.

Kaiden moved fast like lighting and grabbed Zy'Asiah and Ariel, wrapping his arms around their waist and jumped out of the way of the smoke bombs. Then the assassin landed on the ground.

"Who the hell is that?" Ariel asked.

"I don't know," Zy'Asiah answered.

Kaiden suggested, "Wearing black leather from head to toe and a white demon mask of death with horns, I will assume. This vampire I can smell is an assassin."

"An assassin?" Ariel said.

Adrianna was still beauty-sleeping from the needle. Shymair watched from the window. Kaiden saw him looking out the window, and he waved his finger, signaling Shymair not to come out of the house. Huffy landed on the assassin's shoulders.

"What did you shoot my sister with?" Kaiden asked.

The assassin answered, "A sleeping needle. She will wake up in the next hour or two."

Then Kaiden asked, "Who are you?"

"Who I am is not important, but why I am here is. I'm here for Prince Kaiden, only you."

Kaiden said quietly to Ariel and Zy'Asiah, "I'm going to draw him away from the house. You two get inside."

The assassin started walking toward them. Ariel looked at Kaiden and said, "We can take him," and Kaiden said, "No, he's here for me, you will only get in the way."

The assassin approached closer and said, "They can go, I have no business with them."

"Go," Kaiden said to them.

Ariel and Zy'Asiah walked toward the house. Ariel turned around and said, "Kick his ass."

Then the assassin said, "Not here to kill you, Prince Kaiden, here to bring you back."

And Kaiden asked, "Gerald sent you?"

"Yes, I believe he wants to kill you himself now. We can do this the easy way or the hard way, but either way, I get paid."

Kaiden stood in his fighting stance., and the assassin did the same, saying, "The hard way it is." Huffy flew off the assassin's shoulder.

The assassin threw the first punchto Kaiden's face; he blocked it. The assassin struck a second punch; Kaiden grabbed it and back-hand-punched him. The assassin stumbled back and returned with a flying double bicycle kick. Kaiden blocked the kicks. Then the assassin flipped backward in the air, and as he was in the air, he threw a smoke bomb at Kaiden for a distraction, but Kaiden quickly thunderclaps the air of the smoke out. His werewolf fangs tingled a threat, three flying needles coming toward him fast. He quickly bent over backward, flip, dodging the flying needles. The assassin rushed him, they engaged in hand-to-hand combat.

The assassin was hiding a needle under his sleeve. As they were fighting, the assassin waited for the moment to pierce Kaiden in the neck. The assassin slid the needle down in his hand and made his move on Kaiden, but Kaiden punched him in the face. The assassin stumbled back and like a pocket thief, Kaiden quickly removed the needle from his hand. Kaiden spin-kicked the assassin.

He flew ten feet back; his mask cracked. The assassin slowly got up off the ground and said, "This is harder than I thought. Be proud of yourself, Prince Kaiden."

The assassin removed his cracked mask and threw it on the ground. Kaiden was shocked and said, "I know you. You're Seneca... Prince Seneca, the firstborn vampire, son of King Victor Allen, the first to drink the blood of Cain."

"Then you know how powerful I am, Prince Kaiden. I'll show you my true power!"

Seneca transformed; his muscles grew bigger, the leather clothes ripped into shreds, his ears turned pointy like a bat, and his teeth turned razor-sharp. He grew to be six feet, seven inches tall. His skin turned dark. His face turned into a bat-like figure, with long sharp claws, and his eyes turned dark red. Seneca said, "One thing about being a born vampire!"

Seneca stretched both of his arms wide open from his chest and said, "We have abilities!" He formed two fireballs in his hands and smashed the palm of his hands together and blasted fire at Kaiden.

"Shit!" Kaiden said before he flipped sideways, dodging out of the way. He transformed and thunderclapped at Seneca. He dodged out of the way. A few trees were knocked down, you could feel the vibration from the thunderclap under your feet. They charged at each other. Seneca struck a right with his vampire claws, then left, a right, another fight, a left then a left kick. Kaiden caught the kick, holding Seneca's left foot from his ankle, then Seneca backflip-kicked Kaiden in the chin with his right foot. Kaiden stumbled back. Seneca landed on the ground from the backflip. He threw fireballs at Kaiden, but Kaiden quickly caught his balance and dodged the fireballs fast like lightning, you couldn't even see him. Seneca's eyes tried to keep up with him as he continued to throw fireballs at him. Kaiden moved so fast behind him unsurprisingly, Seneca didn't even have the chance to look over his shoulder. Kaiden punch him so damn hard, Seneca flew through Kaiden's house, going through one wall to another, causing Adrianna to wake up in a racing heart, and she said, "*What the hell!*"

Seneca tumbled and rolled, like a skipping rock in a lake. Kaiden jumped high in the air and landed on Seneca's leg, crushing his bone. He declared in a loud, demanding voice, "*You're done!*"

Seneca tried to get up to continue the fight despite his broken leg. Kaiden dared him not to continue. Seneca struck with a right and missed. Kaiden clawed his right arm from his shoulder to his elbow, causing Seneca to lose feeling in his arm. His arm dangled like a swinging rope from a tree. Seneca struck again with a left and missed. Kaiden clawed his right arm and sliced across Seneca's chest, his wounds were cut deep, blood gushing out. Kaiden kicked him, and he flew, hitting his back into a tree, slithering down from the tree like a slug. Seneca turned back to normal, weak and covered in blood, catching his breath.

As Kaiden approached him while he turned back to normal, Seneca looked at him and said with a heavy breath, "Finish me."

"No…I will not, we're alike, you and I."

"How so?" he asked.

And Kaiden said, "Our father exiled us both for being in love with the opposite of our own kind. Abomination, they name that love. You were in love with a human slave woman, and your punishment was to watch her burn from a hanging cross upside down."

As blood gushed out of his mouth, he tried to speak with words, "She was pregnant with twins. I placed my hand on her womb, felt my babies growing, heard their heartbeat. One boy, one girl. The first of their kind, half-human, half-vampire." Seneca looked away, tears from his eyes rolled down his cheeks, and he said, "An abomination to Yeshua, my father yelled out. I fought my father. And lost."

Then Shymair and Adrianna came out of the house.

Seneca looked at Ariel and then back at Kaiden. He said, "I tell you, you're stronger than my father, and with that, be the hope for monsters like us. No more stories of being punished for loving someone. It's a blessing you are in love with a vampire woman."

"There's a jar of blood under the bed, drink it to heal."

Huffy could feel Seneca's emotions and landed on his shoulder.

Kaiden turned around and walked away. He approached Shymair, Zy'Asiah, Ariel, and Adrianna.

"Are you all right?" Ariel asked.

He looked at her and said, "Yes, I'm fine, we should get going."

Shymair smiled and said with excitement, "Now we can finally go to the Oak. I'm starving."

"Hahaha, let us be on our way," Kaiden said.

"What about him, big brother? The assassin," Zy'Asiah asked.

"Seneca is no threat, let him be."

Shymair, Adrianna, and Zy'Asiah walked toward the horse wagon. Shymair climbed on top to steer; the girls climbed on the back. Kaiden and Ariel walked toward their horse buggy. He opened the door for Ariel, then he climbed onto the horse buggy. "Let's go!" Kaiden yelled out.

When they left, Seneca sent Huffy to get the jar of blood from under the bed. Huffy did so and brought it back to him. He drank the blood, and his wounds healed. "Thank you, Prince Kaiden."

## Moments later

They finally arrived at the Oak. They dismounted from the horse wagon and buggy and walked inside. "Finally, we're here," Shymair said.

"Let's take our seats," Zy'Asiah said.

As they were walking toward their table, a familiar face was very happy to see them: the wino. "Friends!" he yelled out happily. "Come, sit, sit, sit, sit," the wino said as he was pulling out their chairs. They sat down and said, "Thank you."

The wino reached his hand across the table with his fingers stretched wide open and a huge smile on his face from ear to ear. He whispered out loud, "Tip."

Shymair handed the wino a coin.

"Yippee!" the wino shouted in enjoyment. Kaiden got up and ordered their food, patiently waiting for it to be done cooking.

A few moments later, they were done eating, and they left the Oak. Standing outside, Shymair rubbed his belly and said, "That was delicious."

"It sure was, cousin," Adrianna said.

With their tummies full and satisfied, a man on a horse wearing silver body armor, werewolves' and vampires' weakness to silver, had hooked to his waist a crossbow that could shoot rapidly with silver arrows, a silver sword on his back with words carved on the sword that said, "Yahweh with Us." The man had a right silver wrist blade and a belt of holy water bombs. The man approached them with fifty bright light soldiers behind him, and he said, "Stop right there!" as he dismounted from the horse.

He approached closer, and Kaiden asked, "How may I help you?"

"It's you that can help me," the man said.

Adrianna asked the man, "How can we help you?"

"My name is Dorian J. Butler, known as Doughboy. I'm the commander and head general of the Bright Light' army. My soldiers came to me and pointed out that you are Prince Kaiden of Galloway. Is this true?"

Kaiden answered, "I am, but what business do you have with me? I am no threat to your kingdom or my people."

Doughboy folded his arms and said, "I received a distress letter from the Kingdom of Vineland. King Booker is dead, and his wife is accused of the crime. The people of the land of Vineland are slaves, forced to work in the gold mines under the sword of King Gerald of Galloway." Doughboy looked at Kaiden with a stern face and said, "He is your uncle, is he not?"

"Blood doesn't make us family," Kaiden said aggressively.

Then Adrianna said, "That bastard killed our father and mother and stole the kingdom!"

Doughboy placed his hands on his hips and said, "I assumed you knew of this, but it seems you do not. Your words make sense, but I don't believe Queen Hannah killed her husband, that doesn't make sense. What makes sense, King Gerald had the king killed, and he had the king's wife take the blame, forced the people into slavery, and now the people of Vineland cry out for help. It's my duty to help. Prince Kaiden, I hear rumors of you being the legendary primordial werewolf, to bring hope to Yeshua's people. Are you a man of the all-knowing Yeshua?"

125

"Yeshua is the way," Kaiden answered.

"Then shall we travel as allies and help me free the people?" Doughboy asked.

"Yes. If you don't mind traveling with four werewolves and a vampire?" Kaiden asked.

Doughboy looked at them and said, "I see no monsters here." Then Doughboy asked, "Where are you traveling first?"

"The Wolf Clan," Kaiden said.

"I know of that place, Lord Shummy's land."

Then Shymair said, "He is my father."

"We can set up camp there. Kaiden and Shummy's son, lead the way, and let us leave now before the gray clouds open and your vampire is burnt to death," Doughboy said.

Then Kaiden, Adrianna, Shymair, Zy'Asiah, and Ariel walked toward their horse wagon and buggy, and they all traveled off, leaving the kingdom of Bridgeton.

## Three days later of traveling together

On their travel, Shymair led the way on the path, riding the horse wagon with the girls sitting at the back, the Bright Light soldiers on their horses traveling behind them in a line of four. Kaiden traveled in the middle of them, riding the horse buggy, while Ariel was comfortable inside, reading her book and drinking a jar of human blood. Doughboy rode behind Kaiden, galloping on the side of him, and said, "May we have a conversation?"

Kaiden looked at him and said, "Yes, and there is something I would like to ask you."

"Speak your peace," Doughboy replied.

"How did you get the nickname Doughboy?"

He laughed a little and said, "My mother and father own a bakery named Doughboy, selling the best cookies and cakes in the Kingdom of Bridgeton. When I was a little boy, people in the community knew me as Doughboy. Miss Ruth, who oversaw the Catholic church kitchen, was the first one to name me that when I dropped off the desserts, and the name stuck with me."

"Interesting," Kaiden said, and then he asked, "How did you become the commander of the Bright Light army?"

"Ah, my father was the commander. I trained under him for a few years, and then I trained in the camps, working my way up through the ranks, fighting hundreds of my men at a time, ten a week, sometimes twenty. Even werewolves and vampires, under the law of the church."

"You followed in your father's footprints," Kaiden said.

"Don't we all? My wife and I own my father and mother's bakery store. Now I'll ask you a question."

"Go on."

"Is it true that werewolves are connected to the spirit of nature?"

Kaiden answered, "Yes. Only the born ones. It's not easy. You must physically train your mind. I only connected one time, and that was by accident. I struggled, and I haven't put in the time."

Then Doughboy asked, "What are your intentions when your eyes lay upon your uncle?"

"I'm going to drive a sword through his chest."

"Then you may use mine."

Doughboy and Kaiden talked a bit longer until they found a suitable spot to set up camp for the night. They rested and enjoyed a meal and drinks. They sat by the fire, and some soldiers were already asleep in their camps. Doughboy relaxed by the fire with Shymair, Adrianna, and Zy'Asiah, while Kaiden kept Ariel company in the horse buggy. She said to him as he held her, "There's something I must tell you, it's been weighing on my mind heavily."

He looked at her with concern and said, "What is it, my love?"

"The day we spoke with your father, I recognized your uncle. He came to my father to stage a fake war to kill your father. I'm sorry, please forgive me, my love. When I recognized him, I didn't know what to say at the time. Your father was yelling and screaming, and I said to myself, 'Shit, I knew this plan wasn't going to work.' But it did, and you paid the price."

He gently rubbed her cheek and looked deeply into her eyes. "Do you love me?" he asked.

"With my God-given heart," she replied.

"Then all is forgiven," he said.

They kissed and ended their night, but as they dozed off, Kaiden had his hand on her stomach and said, "My love, I can feel a heartbeat inside of you."

"I'm pregnant."

He replied with a smile, "Oh, shit. I'm going to be a father." Then they dozed off.

The next morning, everyone woke up and gathered their things to begin the journey. Kaiden and Ariel shared the good news of the new member of the family with everyone. His sisters and his cousin were happy for them, and Doughboy said, "I'm glad I was here to hear that."

Moments later, they were back on the path.

## Four days later

The day was night, and after a long journey of traveling, they finally made it to the Wolf Clan Warrior. Shymair said, "Open the gate, I'm home!"

The lookout guard opened the gate and yelled out, "Shymair and the others have returned!"

Doughboy told his men to wait there when they entered inside. They dismounted from the horse wagon and buggy. Shummy walked toward them, and Adrianna and Zy'Asiah ran to him with open arms. They hugged emotionally, and he said, "I prayed for y'all safety."

Kaiden and Shymair approached Shummy, and Shymair said, "I missed you, Father." They hugged, and Shymair asked, "Where is mother?"

Shummy replied, "She's inside, resting."

Shummy looked at Kaiden and said, "Nephew, get over here." They hugged, and as they embraced each other, Shummy said, "The prince has come home."

Then he looked at Ariel and said, "Young lady, we are family here." They hugged.

Shummy then asked, "Who is your friend here? With his soldiers outside my gate."

Kaiden introduced, "This is Doughboy, the General Commander of the Bright Light Army."

They shook hands, and Shummy said, "I know of you. I've heard of your skills, of you being an excellent fighter. What is your business here?"

"To free the people of Vineland."

Shummy continued, "Let us sit by the fire. We must talk, all of us."

They all sat by the fire, and Shummy started the conversation by saying, "While y'all were out looking for Kaiden and making new friends, I had my people snooping around. After Gerald killed his brother and my sister-in-law, he made himself the new king of Galloway."

"Not surprised," Zy'Asiah said.

Shymair added, "The people of Vineland are slaves. He has many guards making the people work in the gold mines. Queen Hannah is locked up in the dungeon, starving her to death."

"Darn it!" Doughboy exclaimed. He asked Shummy, "Who's in charge?"

Shummy looked at him and answered, "General Werewolf Vegeta and his army are ruling the land of Vineland, under the command of King Gerald."

"I will have Vegeta's head on my sword in the name of Yeshua, I will!" Doughboy declared.

Shummy turned to Ariel and said, "Ariel."

"Yes," she answered. Shummy paused for a second, staring at her in distress for words. Ariel said to him, "Why do you suddenly look worried?"

Finally, Shummy said, "Your father, King Philip...is dead. His life is gone."

She shook her head and said, "No. No, that's impossible."

Shummy said, "I'm sorry, he is gone. That traitor Gerald had him killed."

"Damn it," Doughboy said.

"Honey, everything will be all right," Kaiden said, trying to comfort her. She got up and walked off with tears rolling down her eyes. Adrianna said, "This is really sad."

Kaiden got up and went after her, walking behind her, and approached her slowly. He grabbed her from behind, wrapping his arms around her waist, and said, "It's okay not to be okay and cry." He kissed her on the side of the cheek, and she said, "I'm not just crying because his life is gone. Our last moment together was unpleasant, and I have to carry that burden."

He turned her around, gently grabbed her by the chin, and looked deep into her eyes. He said, "We carry that burden together."

She said, "Yes, my love, together." He wiped her tears and kissed her on the forehead. She laid her head on his chest. Then Shummy, Shymair, and the others approached them, but Doughboy stayed by the fire.

Shummy said, "It's hard now, but it will get easier."

"Yes," she said and then asked, "Is our old shack house available?"

Shummy answered, "It's always available for you and Kaiden."

"Thank you, Uncle Shummy," Ariel said. Then she looked at Kaiden and said, "My love, I'm going to rest for tonight." She looked at Shymair and the girls and said, "Good night to all."

Adrianna said, "Good night," and Zy'Asiah said, "Sleep well."

Ariel walked toward their shack house and went inside. "I hope she'll be okay," Shymair said with concern.

Doughboy got up and approached them. Kaiden looked at them and said, "This madman must be stopped at once."

"Agreed," Doughboy said. Then he continued, "We must free the people of Vineland."

"Yes, of course. You and I, along with your men, will leave tomorrow night. They will suffer no more."

Shummy said, "Ten of my men will join as well." He looked at Adrianna and Zy'Asiah and said, "Girls, you will stay here with Ariel."

Kaiden concluded, "Then it's settled. We end our night and prepare for tomorrow night for the people of Vineland." They ended their night, Shummy put out the fire, and Shymair went to keep his mother company before ending his night. When the fire was put out, Shummy followed behind his son. Doughboy returned to his men, and they set up camp outside the walls. Kaiden went inside the shack house with Ariel and lay down with her in bed. The girls retired for the night.

# Chapter 10

# I Love You, Son

The new day had come, and they waited until nightfall. When night arrived, with the moon shining bright, Shummy's men, Kaiden, Doughboy, and his men mounted their horses and rode swiftly to reach the land of Vineland.

Hours later, they finally arrived in Vineland. Positioned atop a hill, they scouted the area and were horrified to see people locked in cages like filthy, dirty animals, with barely any food to eat.

"This is horrible," Doughboy said as he looked through binoculars.

"I count just about forty-five soldiers, a few of them patrolling back and forth, guarding the area," Kaiden said.

One of Doughboy's scouts approached them and said, "On the other side, I count fifty-five."

"That's about a hundred werewolf soldiers," Doughboy said as he continued to look through the binoculars and said, "Now, where is that bastard, Vegeta?" Doughboy spotted Vegeta walking in the castle and said, "There's the dog."

Then Kaiden said to Doughboy, "I'll sneak in quietly, cut a few throats along the way, and free the people. Wait for my signal and rush in, like an angry mob."

"What's your signal?" he asked.

Kaiden looked at him and replied, "You'll know when I know."

"That's helpful."

Kaiden left the hill while Doughboy and his men, as well as Shummy's men, waited for Kaiden's unknown signal. He slowly crept in, quietly behind a guard, his claws razor-sharp. As he got closer behind the guard, Kaiden ripped the guard's throat out, and he moved on quickly and quietly, leaving the guard's body on the ground. He did the same to another guard, ripping out his throat. Kaiden hid behind a wall, waiting for another guard to pass by. Kaiden came from behind him and ripped his throat out. Kaiden picked up the guard's bow and his arrows. He moved on fast and quiet, and he stretched the bow and released the arrow, shooting the guard in the head.

He moved on and saw the people in cages, with five guards. Kaiden shot the first one in the eye, causing him to fall to his knees. Kaiden shot the guard again in the throat and moved quietly and swiftly around the second one. Kaiden shot him in the chest and again in the throat. Kaiden ran out of arrows, so he took the dagger from one of the dead guards. He crept slowly behind the third guard and stabbed him repeatedly in the throat. Kaiden then threw the dagger at the fourth guard's chest, and as the guard fell, Kaiden ran toward him, pulled the dagger out of his chest, and stabbed him in the side of the neck. He made it to where the people were held captive.

"Free us, please!"

"Free us!"

"Let us flee from here!"

Kaiden, with his werewolf strength, ripped the locks off the cages and said, "*Go! Have your freedom!*"

The fifth guard sees him freeing the people and said, "Damn!" The guard transformed into a werewolf. Kaiden transformed as well and tore his arm off, picking the armless guard up above his head and throwing him so far in the air that one of Shummy's men pointed and said, "Something's flying toward us." The armless werewolf guard landed near Doughboy and his soldiers, and he said, "That's the signal! Let's go!"

Doughboy, on his horse leading his soldiers into battle, with Shummy's men following behind them, transformed into werewolves. As they charge into battle, the slaves ran out, and Doughboy said, "The five of you, get the people to safety!"

The battle began, with Kaiden killing many. Doughboy's soldiers swung their silver swords while Shummy's men used their claws. Doughboy dismounts from his horse and ran into the castle. Kaiden followed behind him, and Doughboy said to Kaiden, "No, my friend! You free the queen, General Vegeta is mine."

Kaiden turned back to normal and asked, "Is this personal?"

And he said, "It's for three reasons why I wish to kill this monster. Free the people, restore honor to the queen," and then he said with passion, "and avenge my brother's murderer!"

Kaiden placed his hand on Doughboy's shoulder and said, "Fight well, my friend, in the name of Yeshua."

They departed, and Kaiden ran toward the downstairs dungeon, while Doughboy made his way to the king's hall. When he arrived at the door, he unsheathed his silver sword and burst through the doors, saying, "I'm here to fucking end you, Vegeta."

And Vegeta said, "Cut the bullshit of your horse shit...General Commander Dorian J. Butler. You're here for revenge of me killing your pathetic, useless-ass brother, Anthony. You should be thanking me, you dumb fool. His death is the reason why you are in his place."

He pointed his sword at him and said, "You took my brother's life, now I will take yours."

"Make your move, Doughboy!" Then Vegeta transformed into a werewolf and rushed toward him.

Doughboy dodged out of the way and threw a firebomb at him, causing Vegeta to flip backward in the air. Vegeta got up and moved quickly on Doughboy, but Doughboy threw his daggers at Vegeta. He dodged the throwing daggers and struck with his claws across Doughboy's chest. The silver armor protected him, and it did not damage him. Doughboy swung his sword, cutting off Vegeta's right arm. Vegeta kicked him, and he impacted into the wall. Vegeta used his left arm to grab a chair and threw it at him. In the nick of time, Doughboy rolled out of the way of the throwing chair and threw two daggers at him, flying toward him like bullets. The daggers pierced him in the arm as he covered his face for blocking.

Doughboy rushed toward him and struck with his sword. Vegeta dodged back from the swing of the sword and backhand-punched Doughboy in the face and struck him again straight in the face with a punch. Doughboy stumbled, then caught his balance and swung his sword, but with Vegeta's one good arm, he caught the swing of the sword. He grabbed Doughboy's sword and threw the sword away from him. But Doughboy quickly jumped and with two feet kicked Vegeta in the chest. He stumbled back, and Doughboy rolled away and unsheathed two of his silver wrist blades. He charged at Vegeta like a raging bull and swung a right near his chest and swung a left near his neck and another right by his neck. Vegeta punched him on the side of his face. Doughboy spun around and aimed his wrist blade like a shooting arrow at Vegeta. With his thumb, he squeezed the trigger, releasing the silver blade off his wrist. The blade flew off his wrist like an arrow and pierced Vegeta below the collarbone. With his other wrist blade, Doughboy shot him again, piercing Vegeta's right foot; he could not move. Then Doughboy ran toward him in a fiery rage, grabbed a firebomb off his belt, and said, "*This is for my brother!*"

He ran, then slid and dropped the firebomb under Vegeta's legs. *Boom!* Blood and guts were everywhere. Half of Vegeta's body blew up. He was crawling on the floor, bleeding out. Doughboy walked toward his sword and picked it up. From behind, he slowly approached Vegeta as he was crawling on the floor to get away. With Doughboy's two hands, he raised his sword and stabbed Vegeta in the head. He was now dead.

## Meanwhile

Kaiden went down to the dungeon, and Queen Hannah heard someone coming. She was weak and could barely move or speak. She asked with a low voice, "Who is there?"

He approached her cell door and said, "It is I, Prince Kaiden. I am here to free you." Kaiden opened her cell door and said, "You have nothing to worry about."

She looked up at him and said, "I prayed for someone like you to come."

He helped her up, and she tried to walk, and she said, "I believe I can manage."

They left the dungeon and headed outside the castle. Doughboy followed behind them, and Kaiden asked him, "Good fight?"

He replied, "Good fight."

Then Doughboy said to Queen Hannah, "My queen, I am Dorian J. Butler, the general commander of the Bright Light Army of the Catholic church. Kaiden and I have restored your kingdom, and under the church, your name shall be cleared."

She said, "Thank you, thank you."

As they walked outside the castle, the battle was over and won. Shummy's men, Doughboy's soldiers, and the freed slaves of Vineland saw Queen Hannah coming out of the castle doors. Doughboy said to the people, "This woman has been falsely accused of a crime by King Gerald of Galloway. She is innocent and still your queen. Honor her!"

The people shouted with joy. They were no longer slaves, and the queen had regained her kingdom.

## Later that night

Doughboy and his men, along with Shummy's men and Kaiden, returned to the Wolf Clan Warrior. The tower guard saw them coming and opened the big wooden gates so they could enter inside. When they entered, Shummy, Shymair, Kim, Adrianna, Zy'Asiah, and Ariel approached them as they were coming. Ariel hugged Kaiden and said to him, "My love, you have returned to me."

He kissed her and replied, "Of course, I have."

Shummy walked toward Kaiden, placed his hand on Kaiden's shoulder, and said, "You are a good man, nephew."

Shummy looked at Doughboy and said, "Thank you for your help."

They shook hands, and Doughboy replied, "The pleasure is mine, General Shummy."

Kim hugged Kaiden and said, "I'm proud of you, my nephew."

Shymair picked up Kaiden and yelled, "*Hell yeah!*"

Kaiden laughed and said, "All right, put me down."

Both of his sisters embraced him, and Adrianna said, "I'm glad you made it back," while Zy'Asiah said, "Me too, little brother."

Doughboy's men returned to their camps by the walls, and they all walked over to the fire. When they arrived by the fire, Kaiden turned around, looked at them, and said, "I am proud of you all. You have all done well. By tomorrow, Gerald will have word of tonight. He will be dead by then. Tomorrow, we attack and restore the kingdom of Galloway."

Kim said, "Your father and my sister would be proud of you!"

Doughboy said, "You have my sword!"

"I stand with you!" Adrianna said.

"So do I!" Zy'Asiah said.

"I fight with you, cousin!" Shymair said.

"And I fight with you, nephew!" Shummy said.

Ariel looked at him and said, "I'm with you, my love."

Kaiden looked at them and said, "We attack tomorrow night."

After they were done, Doughboy approached Shummy and said to him, "I'll keep my men here to protect your people and wife while we battle."

Shummy said, "Are you sure?"

Doughboy looked at Kaiden and said to Shummy, "We have the best weapon."

"Indeed, we do."

They retired for the night. Doughboy went outside the walls and slept in his tent while Shummy and his wife, Kim, went into their house. Kaiden's sisters did the same. Ariel and Kaiden ended their night in the shack house.

Shymair stayed by the fire.

## *The next day*

At the kingdom of Galloway Castle, King Gerald sat at the table eating his morning meal. As he was feasting, his consulting approached him and said, "My king, I'm sorry to disturb you, but I must inform you that the Kingdom of Vineland has been overrun. The people have taken back their land and freed the queen."

King Gerald stopped eating, closed his eyes as he was frustrated with patience, and he asked, "Where the hell is General Vegeta?"

He answered, "He is dead, my king."

King Gerald got up from the table, walked toward the window with his hands folded behind his back, and asked, "Who's responsible for this?"

"Commander Doughboy, with the help of Kaiden, my king."

The king turned around from the window and said, "No matter. I have collected enough gold. The Kingdom of Vineland is no longer a concern to us."

King Gerald walked away from the window, sat back down in his chair, and said, "My nephew will come for me. I can only imagine his rage. Have my men ready and guards standing outside the castle. I believe war is coming." The king continued to eat his morning meal, and his consulting left him to be.

## Back at the Wolf Clan Warrior

Hours later, night came, and they were preparing for tonight's attack. Everyone gathered together, ready to fight. Kaiden said to them all, "Tonight, the Kingdom of Galloway will be restored, and we shall overthrow the devil himself from the throne he stole from my father." They cheered and yelled, and Kaiden continued, "I am grateful for everyone, giving their lives for the kingdom! I honor you all."

Doughboy yelled out, "*We fight with you!*"

Shymair said, "Time to fight!"

"*For Father!*" Adrianna said.

Zy'Asiah said, "And for the kingdom!"

*One hour later, at midnight*

Kaiden looked at the full moon and said, "The white moon."

Then he walked toward Ariel, who was sitting on the steps of their shack house, drinking a jar of human blood before the battle began. He approached and said, "My love?"

She put the jar down, got up, and said, "Yes?"

He held her hand and gave her a red rose he had picked from outside the walls. He looked deep into her eyes and asked, "Will you marry me?"

With tears in her eyes and joy, she said, "*Yes!*" He was happy with her answer, and he kissed her.

Adrianna and Zy'Asiah approached them. "Why the tears?" Zy'Asiah asked.

"We are engaged!" Ariel said.

"*What!* When?" Adrianna asked as she was in shock.

"Just now," Kaiden said.

They hugged her and said, "This is wonderful news. My new sister-in-law."

Then it was time for Kaiden, Ariel, Zy'Asiah, Adrianna, Shymair, Shummy, and Doughboy to leave for battle. Doughboy's men and Shummy's men, along with his wife Kim, were ordered and told to stay behind to protect their land from any enemies, as Doughboy had said, "Have the best weapon."

The sky was clear, and the stars were bright, for some said that the angels were watching over them in the name of Yeshua. They made it to the Kingdom of Galloway. Doughboy looked through his binoculars and said, "There are a hundred outside the castle walls, like they knew we were coming."

Shymair used his wolf eyes to take a look and said, "I see about eighty guards in the castle, but no Gerald."

"He must be in the throne room," Kaiden said.

Shymair asked Kaiden, "How are we doing this?"

And he answered, "Like angry dogs." He looked at Ariel and said, "And a vampire." Then he looked at Doughboy and said, "Besides, it appears they know we are coming."

Doughboy responded, "Well, let them see us coming."

Ariel unsheathed both of her wrist blades, her eyes turned dark red, and she said, "Kill them all."

Then Doughboy unsheathed his sword from his back. They charged toward the castle, Ariel riding on her horse, yelling with those dark-red scary eyes.

Doughboy rode on his horse, screaming out loud, "For the people!"

Kaiden, Zy'Asiah, Adrianna, Shummy, and Shymair ran faster than Doughboy and Ariel's horses. On foot, they transformed into werewolves. The guards outside the castle walls saw them coming and warned the tower guard to ring the alarm bell. King Gerald was in the throne room, sitting in the royal chair, and heard the alarm bell. He said calmly, "He is coming."

With Kaiden's primordial werewolf speed, he ran faster than them and jumped eighty feet in the air. He landed and unleashed the biggest thunderclap attack on the werewolf guards, who flew back, killing most of them.

Ariel flipped off her horse, striking with her wrist blades, cutting off limbs. Doughboy swung his sword, chopping off heads. Shummy killed as many as he could, his son Shymair followed with his werewolf claws, covered in the guards' blood. Doughboy and Kaiden stormed into the castle like a hurricane. Adrianna and Zy'Asiah fought the guards outside the castle with Shummy, Shymair, and Ariel.

Kaiden threw the guards around like paper, and Doughboy followed behind him, swinging his sword and throwing firebombs. A group of werewolf guards blocked the hallway. Doughboy took cover behind Kaiden as he thunderclapped the guards out of the way. Doughboy then threw three firebombs, which exploded, splattering blood and guts all over the walls. They continued to storm through, and they finally made it to the throne room by the door.

Kaiden turned back to normal, and Doughboy handed Kaiden his sword. Doughboy said to him, "Good fight," and Kaiden replied, "Good fight." Doughboy stood guard by the door, and Kaiden burst through the doors like an angry raging bull, his eyes dark black and red, filled with hate and rage. His grip was tight on Doughboy's sword. King Gerald got up from the royal chair and could see the angry rage in his nephew. King Gerald raised his hand toward Kaiden and calmly said, "Let me speak, hear my words."

Kaiden heard nothing, as it all fell on deaf ears. King Gerald said, "I am your fat—"

Kaiden moved as fast as lightning, and before King Gerald even had the chance to finish his sentence, Kaiden drove the sword into him below his chest and pulled the sword out. King Gerald spit blood out of his mouth, lost his balance, and gripped Kaiden tightly. As King Gerald was falling to the floor, he uttered the words, "I am your father."

Kaiden's eyes turned back to normal as he was in shock of what he had just heard. He asked, "What's this you speak?"

King Gerald's eyes were tearing, and he said, "It's true, my son. I am your father."

Kaiden could not believe him and said, "You speak lies."

"Ask your mother, she knows the truth."

"You murdered my mother!"

King Gerald, slowly dying, said, "Why would I kill the woman I love, the one promised to me to bear my child? No, son, she lives. She's locked in the tower. I locked her there until things calmed down and I was able to explain myself to you. The key is in my chambers, in the drawer... Free her."

Then Kaiden said, "No, you had the assassin to kill us."

"He was only to bring you back...home, my son."

Kaiden paused for a moment and thought about what the assassin had said before the battle. "Not here to kill you, Prince Kaiden, here to bring you back."

Then Kaiden said, "What of the people of Vineland you enslaved?"

King Gerald tried to say with a slow breath, "Queen Hannah... planned, her idea. I helped her plan come into existence...but I betrayed her, so she could be accused of the crime of the king."

Kaiden dropped the sword and fell on his knees on the floor as he cried. He looked up and said loudly in a distressful crying voice, *"Eli, be merciful on him!"*

141

King Gerald was pale and white. He looked up and saw a bright light shining on him. He saw a man in the middle of that light and said in tears, "Yahweh?" Then he said, "My brother has taken everything from me, my kingdom, my woman, and my child. And now…I forgive my brother." Then King Gerald looked at Kaiden as tears rolled down from his eyes, dropping from his chin, and with his last breath, he said, "I love you, son."

King Gerald closed his eyes, and his soul left his body. Kaiden yelled and screamed in pain. He grabbed the sword and got up. When he looked up, he saw the consulting coming toward him with the key in his hand. Kaiden asked, "You knew?"

He handed Kaiden the key and answered, "Yes."

Kaiden said, "And you spoke of nothing."

"It's not my place to speak, it's my place to serve the heart of men."

Kaiden said, "I can feel your aura has changed, it's different. What the hell are you!"

Then Shymair, Adrianna, Ariel, Doughboy, Shummy, and Zy'Asiah entered the throne room. Kaiden turned his head over his shoulder to look back at them, and when he turned his head back around, the consulting had vanished. They approached Kaiden, and he handed Doughboy back his sword, saying to them, "Mother is alive."

"Alive?" Zy'Asiah said.

"Yes, follow me," Kaiden said.

Afterward, Kaiden and the others went to the tower. As they did, the werewolves' soldiers and guards turned back to normal and kneeled to Kaiden. Then they arrived at the tower. Kaiden looked at them and said, "Stay here, I wish to speak with Mother alone, and I will bring her down."

He went inside the tower and made it to the door, unlocking it with the key. His mother was sitting on the bed. When the door opened, she saw her son, got up, and rushed toward him. They hugged, and as they were hugging, Kaiden said, "Is it true? Did I just murder my father?"

She was in shock, her eyes widened, and she stepped back from him as she gasped for air, covering her mouth. He asked, "You know of this?"

She answered, "Sweetie, you must understand, your father, the late King Ka'Ron, truly loves you."

He said in anger, "He is not my father! Speak, Mother?"

And she said, "Okay. I tell you the truth, it's time you know." She sat on the bed and said, "When I was younger, I was in love with a man, your father, Gerald."

Kaiden eyes were tearing.

And she continued to say, "His brother, Ka'Ron, your real uncle, knew of this, just as well he knew the throne was promised to his brother, Gerald. Your grandfather died in the battle of the second war of vampires and werewolves, freeing the humans from slavery. Ka'Ron somehow manipulated for him to be the king of Galloway. Then my father came to tell me I was now promised to marry Ka'Ron. He was sleeping with multiple women because I could not give him a son. I was hurt and in pain. I went to your father Gerald that night. Ka'Ron sensed you are not his, as evil as that bastard is, he forgave me when I was pregnant with you and told Gerald his punishment would be to raise his son as his own. If any of us spoke of it, we would be put to death. And as you can see, he treated you no differently. Privately, he said to me that he had done enough damage to his brother." Then she looked at Kaiden and said, "You are king now, my son. Make a difference."

He walked toward her, hugged her, and said, "I love you, Mother."

Then they walked out of the tower, and Adrianna and Zy'Asiah were happy with joy to see their mother. They hugged her. Shummy said, "Sister-in-law, it's good to see you." They hugged, and she said, "My brother-in-law."

She looked at Shymair and said, "My nephew." They hugged.

"Auntie," he replied.

Doughboy introduced himself and said, "Queen Lawanda, I am Dorian J. Butler, the commander of the Bright Light Army."

They shook hands, and she said, "Nice to meet you."

Then she looked at them all and said, "Thank you, thank you so much, Kaiden, my girls. I love you all so much."

"I love you, Mother," Zy'Asiah said.

"Woman, you will always have my love," Kaiden said with passion.

## *An hour later*

Kaiden and Doughboy spoke privately outside the walls of Galloway by the mountain. Kaiden said, "I asked to speak with you alone because I have terrible news of what I was told by a dying man." He looked at Doughboy and continued, "Queen Hannah helped participate in having her people as slaves working in the gold mine. Killing her husband was part of the plan, but not being accused of the crime, it was a double-cross by the late King Gerald."

Doughboy was in disbelief and asked, "What evidence is there of this?"

Kaiden replied, "There is none, only words for now."

Doughboy, angered, said, "So she goes unpunished. That bitch! And I believed she was righteous. There must be some proof somewhere."

"What's in the dark shall come to the light. It shall surface," Kaiden said.

"Well, until then, me and my men will travel back home. I will speak highly of you to the leaders of the church."

They hugged, and Kaiden said, "Thank you for your help, my friend."

Doughboy replied, "Good fight."

Kaiden placed his hand on Doughboy's shoulder and said, "Good fight."

After they were done talking, Doughboy said to Kaiden, "Tell the others I said bye. We shall see each other soon." Kaiden returned to the castle where the others waited for him while Doughboy and his men traveled back home.

# Chapter 11

# A New Beginning

One month had passed since they announced Kaiden as the new king of Galloway.

It's a new beginning on this beautiful day, a wedding day in the king's hall. Today, King Kaiden was marrying the love of his life, the new queen of Galloway, Queen Ariel, who was carrying his child. They stand facing each other, holding each other's hands in marriage, being wed by Albert Morgan, the pastor of the Kingdom Bridgeton Church. He said, "My king, your vows." King Kaiden spoke his vows.

After King Kaiden spoke his vows, Pastor Albert said to Queen Ariel, "My lady, your vows."

After she spoke her vows, Pastor Albert looked at King Kaiden and said, "You may kiss the bride." They kiss, and everyone in attendance at the wedding cheered. The newlyweds walked down the aisle as flowers were being thrown. The wedding reception was a joyous celebration. People enjoyed themselves while soldiers stood guard.

King Kaiden and Queen Ariel cut the cake, baked by Doughboy and his wife.

Queen Ariel said as she took a bite, "Thank you for this, Doughboy, and to your lovely wife."

Doughboy replied, "Thank you, my lady."

The king said, "I'm glad you're here."

Doughboy said, "Thank you for the invite."

Queen Helen approached her daughter and her new son-in-law, and she said, "I know your father may have disapproved of your new life, but as your mother, I'm proud of you, my daughter."

Queen Ariel said, "Thank you, Mother." They hugged, and Queen Helen said to King Kaiden, "Take care of her."

"I will."

As the music was playing, Adrianna and Zy'Asiah approached them.

"Brother?" Adrianna said.

"And sister-in-law," Zy'Asiah said.

"Shall we dance?" Adrianna asked.

"We shall," they answered. They danced on the dance floor.

Then Lawanda approached and said to King Kaiden, "May I have this dance with my son."

And he said, "Yes, you may." And he danced with his mother.

After they danced, Shummy and his wife, Kim, said, "Newlyweds! Newlyweds! Come open the gifts!"

Shymair said, "Yes, let's see the goodies!"

King Kaiden and Queen Ariel opened their gifts, and one particular gift stood out the most: a strange purple box. Kaiden opened the box and saw it was Gerald's handwritten letter to the assassin, detailing Queen Hannah's plot against her king.

He quickly handed the letter to Doughboy and said, "We have our proof."

Doughboy read the letter and then said, "What's in the dark shall come to the light, as you said."

The assassin was watching from afar and was happy King Kaiden received the letter, and then he left. They continued to enjoy the rest of the wedding reception.

## One week later

Soldiers of the Bright Light Army marched through the Kingdom of Vineland with an arrest warrant for Queen Hannah. She knew of their coming, the castle doors were locked as Doughboy banged on them He ordered his men to kick the doors down. With a burst open, they marched through the castle.

In the throne room, Queen Hannah knelt with the doors locked, clutching a knife to her throat, praying to Yeshua for forgiveness. Doughboy and his men tore down the throne room door, and he saw the queen with the knife dangerously close to her neck. He yelled, *"Put the knife down!"*

Before they had a chance to reach her, she cut her own throat.

The Kingdom of Vineland was under the protection of the Kingdom of Bridgeton. The Kingdom of Vineland, with no king and queen, now belonged to the church.

## Two weeks later

King Kaiden sat in his throne chair when a guard approached him and said, "My king, you have someone who wishes to speak with you."

"Who may it be?" the king asked.

The guard answered, "King Richard's daughter, Princess Faith."

"Let her in," the king said.

The guard left, and she entered the room. King Kaiden asked her, "What brings you to me?"

She replied, "I'm not here to cause trouble or to sow discord between you and your new bride. I understand you denied my hand in marriage because destiny chose otherwise in love for you. I have no choice but to accept that. But I'm not here to explain how my heart is broken. I'm here to warn you, King Kaiden."

He inquired, "And what is this warning?"

"My father is very angry with you for denying my hand in marriage for a vampire woman, and you know, as I know, that is an abomination according to the law of the elders. He's planning war on you with his allies. They're coming for you, King Kaiden."

He said, "Let them come. I will defeat them all."

"Indeed you shall. My blessings to you and your new bride, and your child, the first of its kind—half vampire, half werewolf. I may leave you now."

As Princess Faith was leaving, King Kaiden said, "*Wait!*" He got up from his throne chair, walked toward her, and said, "Thank you."

She smiled and then lft.

### Eighth months and two weeks had passed

The moon was full and bright, and on this night, Queen Ariel was giving birth. King Kaiden waited patiently with his sisters. They could see he was nervous as he sat and shook his leg. Zy'Asiah comforted him and said, "Everything's going to be all right."

Adrianna said, "Yes, brother, be strong."

"I'm trying to hold on, but I can hardly bear it," he said.

In the room where the queen was delivering the baby, "Push, my lady, push!" the midwife said as she held her hand.

And the other midwife said, "The baby is crowning!"

Lawanda used cold rags to keep her at ease. "The baby is almost here, keep pushing," her mother-in-law said as she continued to place cold rags, and she said, "You can do it, push Grandma's baby out."

The midwife pulled the baby out and said, "It's a boy!" She handed the baby to its mother, and her first words to her son were, "He really does have hair."

Lawanda left the room to inform her son and her two daughters. She walked into the room and said, "My son."

He looked at her and said, "Yes, Mother?"

She said, "You have a son, and I have a grandson, the new prince of Galloway."

He was excited and rushed toward her. He walked into the room. Queen Ariel held the baby.

He approached and said, "My boy, my beautiful boy."

She asked her husband, "What shall we name him?"

His sisters came into the room behind him. "My nephew," Adrianna said.

"The first of his kind, magnificent," Zy'Asiah said.

The king picked his new son up and held his baby boy as the baby cried. He said, "We shall name him Lucius, which means light. Half werewolf and half vampire. He is the vaelycanthropy."

Printed in the USA
CPSIA information can be obtained
at www.ICGtesting.com
CBHW030135041024
15319CB00043B/397

9 798893 080339